Phantom Horse
In Danger

Phantom Horse
In Danger

Christine Pullein-Thompson

RAVETTE BOOKS

This edition published by Ravette Books Limited 1989

Phototypeset by Input Typesetting Ltd, London
Printed and bound in Great Britain
for Ravette Books Limited,
3 Glenside Estate, Star Road,
Partridge Green, Horsham,
West Sussex RH13 8RA
by Cox & Wyman Ltd,
Reading

ISBN 1 85304 118 1

1

It was the end of March. Easter term had just finished. The garden was full of crocuses and the first daffodils. Upstairs, Mum was packing. I stood in the doorway, watching her.

"I wish you weren't staying alone," she said. "I hate leaving you. Why won't you agree to Aunt Nina staying with you?"

"We're nearly grown-up," replied my brother. "We are not children any more." He was sitting on the bed, nearly six foot tall, with long legs and dark brown hair.

"I've made an important decision," he continued, looking at the floor. "I am going to sell Killarney and buy a moped. I want to be more independent, and I'm sick of mucking out . . ."

There was a terrible, shocked silence. I thought of Killarney going, of his empty loose box, of never seeing him again.

"It is a very sudden decision," replied Mum, shutting her suitcase. "Won't you miss him?"

"Yes, in a way. But one must move forward, one can't stay the same for ever," said Angus.

"But what about the hunter trials?" I asked. "There are three in April."

"I'll ride on my moped and watch you fall off,"

said Angus, with a silly smile on his face which made me want to scream.

"Is it just a matter of money?" asked Mum.

"No. I'm just tired of doing the same things—cleaning tack and mucking out. I want a change. I want oil on my hands instead of horsehair," answered Angus, standing up and stretching. "It's too much responsibility . . ."

"I'll be responsible then," I suggested quickly. "I can easily look after two horses."

"Look, I've written out an advertisement," said Angus, as though I had never spoken, and he took out a piece of paper from his pocket and handed it to me.

I read out aloud:

KILLARNEY: 16 hand Grey Gelding rising six. Marvellous temperament. Super jumper, excellent hunter. Good private home only. No dealers. £2,000 o.n.o.

"How can you?" I cried. "How can you sell him just for a beastly moped? You're not asking enough either. He's worth more than that, much more."

"I want him to have a good home. I don't *want* lots of money. Can't you understand?" shouted Angus.

"No, I can't," I yelled back.

"Can't you understand that a moped won't cost pounds and pounds a week to feed all through the winter, and need a new set of shoes every four weeks? It will be much cheaper for Dad."

"It will need petrol and oil, and new tyres, insurance and licence," I answered. "It will keep going wrong. Mopeds always do. And who will pay for that?"

"Well, I'm not sticking to a moped for ever. As soon as I'm old enough I'm buying a motor bike," shouted Angus. "And I'll get a job. I'll pay for everything."

Mum had her hands over her ears. I ran from the room, down the twisty cottage stairs, out into the sudden March sunshine.

Killarney was grazing under the apple trees, close to my own Phantom. He was starting to lose his winter coat, and looked every inch a hunter, from his large hocks to his wonderful shoulder and his wise, grey Irish head. I could feel tears smarting behind my eyes. I thought, why do people have to change? I wished I could stay my age for ever, that everything could remain just the same, with Phantom grazing in the orchard, and the garden full of flowers. I looked at our small stableyard and imagined a moped, followed by a motor bike, in Killarney's loose box. I thought, soon his head will never look over the door again. I fetched a wheelbarrow and started to muck out, and as I worked I could feel tears trickling down my cheeks.

Later, Mum left, but first she stood in the kitchen, looking at her watch and telling us, "You will be careful, won't you? I'll ring you every night. I hate leaving you on your own. Don't be reckless. Don't leave the lights on when you go to bed. Remember to lock up and to pay the milkman . . ."

"We are not six," replied Angus. "Do stop fussing. We'll be all right. We're nearly grown-up." I didn't touch wood.

"If only you had let Aunt Nina stay here," said Mum, walking down the little path to the garage.

"She's more trouble than she's worth," replied Angus.

"But she's kind and an adult." Mum got into the car and started the engine. I stood waving.

"Come back soon," I shouted. "Give my love to Dad."

"I wish I wasn't going. I don't like entertaining," said Mum, turning down the car window.

"You'll miss your plane in a minute. You know there's always a traffic jam at Heathrow," said Angus "It's three o'clock."

"I'll bring you back Easter eggs—Swiss ones," shouted Mum, driving away.

"She doesn't realise we're grown-up," said Angus.

"I'm not. Are you really selling Killarney?"

"Yes, the advertisement will be in Saturday's *Horse and Hound*."

"You mean you've sent it?"

He nodded. "Once I've taken a decision I don't waste time," he answered in a self-satisfied voice.

The place felt empty and forlorn without Mum. I started wishing that Dad had a different job, that he wasn't in the Foreign Office and constantly abroad. Once we had travelled with him. But now, suddenly, we were all sick of airports and aeroplanes, of missing horse shows and gymkhanas, of never staying long enough at home to make real friends. So Angus and I decided to stay behind rather than be bored in a hotel in Geneva, and now, a week later, Mum was following Dad to help with entertaining. Mrs Parkin was coming in every day to see whether we were still alive and to keep us dusted. The freezer was stocked with food.

Dominic Barnes, who is seventeen, had offered to drive us into the nearest town in his father's Land Rover if we needed anything, and I had bought a diary in which I intended to record everything which happened.

I fetched it now and wrote: *3 p.m. Mum's left. Angus is selling Killarney. I can't believe it. Why do people change? The house seems empty. The stable will seem empty without Killarney. I feel empty too. So will Phantom when Killarney's gone.*

When I went downstairs again, Angus was studying a catalogue of mopeds.

"I'm going to ride. Coming?" I asked.

He shook his head and continued reading.

"Saturday is the day after tomorrow," I said. "Don't you want to ride him as much as possible before he goes?"

"I'm reading," replied Angus. "Who is 'him', anyway?"

I left the house, slamming the back door after me.

Phantom was glad to be caught. He hated doing nothing. I groomed him quickly while Killarney watched us over the gate. Then I tacked him up and set off towards the woods with the sun in my eyes. He jogged and danced, and tossed his head. The trees were breaking into leaf; the woods sparkled with spring. It was like a new beginning. I wanted to sing but the words stuck in my throat. Later on I sang sad hymns like 'Abide with me' and 'Lead kindly light.'

I saw my childhood ending and wondered whether I would ever grow tired of Phantom and

9

want something else instead. It seemed impossible, but I might change like Angus. What then?

I cantered through the woods. They smelt of damp earth; soon they would be mauve-blue with bluebells. Everything changes, I thought, even the woods. But it didn't console me.

I rode home on a loose rein and found Angus preparing an elaborate meal in the kitchen.

"I thought we would have a high tea for a change," he said. "You know, cakes and biscuits and any old thing you can find. I've opened some sardines and there's gherkins and pickle, tinned peaches and three different kinds of bread . . . We can eat everything off the same plate. Are you cross, or something? Why don't you speak?"

"I don't like Killarney going," I answered. "He's such a kind, honest horse. He deserves a good home."

"Do you consider we are such a good home?" asked Angus, sitting down to his high tea.

"Reasonable."

"Don't be silly, we're a jolly boring home. When did we last hunt, for instance? And he loves hunting. He was born for it, it's in his blood. Soon I shall be doing exams. I shan't have any time then. It's kinder to let him go now, while he's in the prime of life. I shall make sure it's a good home, too. I'm not a fiend, Jean . . ." He went on, trying to convince me. "I am *not* a good home, not now, not when I've got exams ahead."

"You could lend him . . ."

"There's no point. I'm giving up riding for the time being," Angus announced, stuffing sardines into his mouth. "I want to learn to drive."

At nine o'clock Mum telephoned from Geneva

to say that she had arrived. "Are you all right?" she asked. "Have you had a proper meal?"

Later, I wandered out into the dark to say good-night to Killarney and Phantom. They nuzzled my pockets and blew in my hair, and I saw that there was a moon riding high and clear in the sky.

I had bedded them down in deep, golden straw. They were warm, content and at home. There was nothing restless about either of them. They looked out calmly and confidently, knowing nothing of what might lie ahead. I wished I was the same, that I could forget tomorrow and the next day.

"Perhaps no one will want you. Why don't you go lame?" I whispered in Killarney's ear. "Then no one will buy you. Then you can stay."

"Kick him," I said to Phantom. "Make him lame . . ."

When I returned to the kitchen, Angus shouted downstairs, "What have you been doing? Lock up, I'm going to bed."

I turned the key on the back door and climbed the stairs, praying. "Please, God, make Killarney lame, just a little, just enough to keep him here.

The next day was Friday. Angus thundered down-stairs at seven o'clock to pick up the local paper from the front doormat. Five minutes later he was calling, "There's a moped for sale. It's quite new and only one hundred and fifty pounds. I shall ask for first refusal."

"You may not sell Killarney. He may go lame or misbehave," I shouted.

"Don't be silly," he replied. "He never goes lame and he never misbehaves . . ."

As I dressed I called to Angus, "Are you riding today? If not I'll have a last ride on Killarney."

Angus replied, "I'm going to ride my bike over to Hillborough and look at the moped. I may not be back to lunch. Don't injure Killarney or ride him too far. I want him in top form tomorrow."

I didn't answer, because suddenly Angus's attitude made me feel sick with rage. Six months ago he had loved Killarney; now he could not wait to sell him—and all for the love of a moped. I couldn't understand how anyone could prefer a machine to a horse, and Killarney was not any old horse, he was young and handsome, without a wicked thought in his head. He had potential, too, the ability to win. He was the sort of horse many people would give all they had to own, and here was Angus rejecting a whole future of hunter trials, horse trials, perhaps even Badminton, for a moped.

I left Phantom in his box and rode Killarney for two hours. Riding him after Phantom was like driving a Rolls after a high-powered sports car, I decided. He wasn't as handy as Phantom, but he had a marvellous stride and his canter was out of this world and, though he was large, he would come back into a walk without pulling.

When I returned home, Angus had gone to view the moped, so I turned the horses out and watched them roll under the apple trees before going indoors to scramble myself eggs for lunch.

Mrs Parkin had arrived and was shaking mats. She was large, motherly and talked a lot.

"What's the matter with Angus this morning, then? He's like a cat on hot bricks," she said.

"He wants a moped and then a motorbike," I said. "He's selling Killarney . . ."

"Boys are all the same, aren't they? First it's mopeds, then it's motor bikes and then a sports car. You can't do anything about it, Jean," she told me.

"I know, but it seems so sad. Killarney was a very special present to Angus. Mum bought him after winning on a Premium Bond. Angus is going to keep the money, and she is too nice to say anything. She won't object, I know she won't, but horses aren't like machines and Killarney's happy here. Once you sell a horse he can end up anywhere," I said. "I never thought Angus would change so quickly. He's so hard now, he just doesn't seem to care."

"We are all changing. You will be just the same soon," said Mrs Parkin. "You'll be thinking of nothing but boys."

"I shall always ride," I answered. "And I shall never sell Phantom. He's part of the family. And as for boys, I shan't think about them until I'm twenty. I want to spend the next five or six years riding. I want to become really good . . ."

"You'll change, you'll see," replied Mrs Parkin, unconvinced, as she switched on the vacuum cleaner.

After lunch I rode Phantom. I schooled him in the paddock which was next to the orchard, practising changes of pace, halting straight, and cantering on either leg, for I planned to ride him in horse trials and his dressage standard was far below his jumping.

Angus arrived home at four.

"Gosh, it was miles," he shouted. "But it's a lovely moped and they are reserving it until

13

Monday. So, if I don't sell Killarney this weekend, I'm sunk."

"There are other mopeds," I answered.

"But they are very hard to find. People just don't sell their mopeds, and this one is in perfect order in every way. I rode it on the road and it was super . . ."

"Once you thought that about Killarney," I answered.

"You do like making me feel guilty, don't you?" answered Angus. "It's not a crime to change."

I hardly slept that night. I imagined people arriving to see Killarney, people we hated on sight. How could we stop them buying him? Neither of us had ever sold a horse before. Suddenly I wished that we were not on our own, that we had our parents to back us up. Dad was a diplomat; he spoke several languages and knew the law inside out, and Mum had a lot of tact. They would have known how to manage unwelcome buyers, but I was on my own for I knew now that I couldn't rely on Angus any more.

He was like someone bewitched, bewitched by the thought of a moped. He had changed beyond all recognition. I got up and looked at my watch. It was five o'clock and cocks were crowing in the distance, heralding another day. By nightfall Killarney could be sold, never to return. It would be a dramatic day—a day we would remember.

2

Angus appeared in my bedroom. "You've over-slept. It's eight o'clock," he said, drawing back the curtains. "I want you to plait Killarney."

"You can want then," I answered.

"Please. I'll pay you."

"I don't want your beastly money. Anyway, who's coming? Has someone rung up?"

"Not yet."

"Exactly. Go away, I want to dress."

"I'll make you a cup of tea if you'll plait him," pleaded Angus.

"No thank you."

"You are going to help, aren't you?" he asked. "I'll need your support. If you say nothing it will look peculiar."

"You are asking a lot," I answered, sitting up. "If it is a good home I may say something, but if the people are ghastly I shall tell them he's broken in the wind."

"Thank you very much," cried Angus, leaving my room and slamming the door after him.

I didn't feel like breakfast. Angus was washing Killarney's tail when I appeared in the stableyard.

"Do you mind listening for the telephone?" he said in a tense voice. "It is important."

"For how long?"

"Ten minutes."

I returned indoors and made myself coffee. The sun shone on the window-panes, showing up the dust. It was April Fool's day, but I didn't feel like making a fool of anyone. I looked at the kitchen clock and started to count the minutes. Then the telephone rang. I picked up the receiver and waited.

"Is that Stour 2324?" asked a man's voice.

"Yes."

"You've advertised a grey gelding for sale. Can we come over and see him at twelve?" he asked.

I wanted to say no. I thought, I could say he's sold, or lame or ill, or that we've changed our minds. But it wouldn't be fair on Angus.

"Well?" said the voice.

"Yes, that's fine. Do you want our address?" I answered. "He's not a novice ride. You know that, don't you?"

"Yes, that's all right. I want him for my son."

I told him our address and asked him for his name. He was called Mr Menzies and he lived on the outskirts of London and would be keeping Killarney at livery near Wimbledon.

I put down the receiver, feeling rather sick. Killarney won't like London after Ireland, I thought. He won't be able to lie in the sun or roll. He will be inside all the time. I hope somebody else rings up.

"Any luck?" asked Angus, returning indoors.

"What luck?" I asked.

"Anybody telephone?"

"Yes. A Mr Menzies. He's arriving at twelve." I told Angus about Wimbledon.

"He won't be bothered with flies in the summer if he's in," said Angus, "and a livery stable will look after him properly. He won't be lonely. He'll have other horses; he'll be all right. You do fuss, Jean; he's only a horse, after all."

Then the telephone rang again. "I'll get it," said Angus. "Find me a pencil and some paper. We must be organised. We don't want to get our customers mixed up." He was smiling now, suddenly sure of getting his moped, while I seemed to be seeing him for the first time, and what I saw I didn't like.

"Stour 2324," he said, sounding businesslike. "Yes, that's right, yes, he's a lovely horse, perfect in every way. He's Irish, yes, he can jump almost anything. No, no trouble to box. Yes, do come. Three o'clock will be fine, but we have got someone else arrivng at twelve. OK eleven, then. Do you want our address? First turn off the motorway, exit nine, then it's ten miles; it's only a hamlet. Fine, see you then. Goodbye . . ."

"She sounded terribly nice," said Angus. "She wants him for horse trials. Are you going to help me get him ready?"

"What about the telephone?" I asked.

"They can ring again later. We've got enough customers for this morning," cried Angus, starting to laugh. "I bet you a pound he's sold by lunch-time."

I found the body brush. Soon we were both covered with grey hairs. When Killarney's mane was glistening in the sun and his legs looked like polished pewter, we rushed indoors to change our clothes.

"I'm sure I've asked too little," cried Angus.

"I should have asked three thousand pounds. I'm a nut-case."

I didn't answer. I could feel a well of sadness inside me. Angus was finishing a chapter of his life without realising it. He was giving up horses. Today was like a farewell. In future I would ride alone, plan my horse shows and other events alone, share my triumphs alone. It was the end of an era.

"But whatever would I do with three thousand pounds?" asked Angus. "I don't want to travel because I've travelled so much already. I suppose I would keep it for my sports car, that's the next thing."

I thought of Mrs Parkin and wondered whether her predictions always came true.

It was now ten-thirty. Angus spent a long time brushing his hair.

"I shall ride him first," he said, "while you put up some jumps and make suitable comments. You know what I mean—a horse in a million, quite unblemished, a child could ride him . . . You know the correct chat, don't you?"

"Don't you care, don't you care at all?" I asked incredulously.

"Not much, not really, you see I want to change. I want a new image. I've been horsey long enough," replied my brother, looking at me seriously with his brown eyes. "After all, how many of our male friends ride?"

"Well, Dominic Barnes, for one," I answered. "He's started point-to-pointing."

"Well, he's a special case. I mean, his father was a National hunt rider before he took up farming. And he's not exactly highbrow, is he? He's always milking or on a tractor. He'll never be Prime Minister."

I had no answer, for now we seemed to be on a different wavelength. The Barneses have always helped us out. They looked after our ponies Moonlight and Mermaid, and Twilight, who is a yearling and belongs to Angus.

"I suppose you'll sell Twilight next," I said.

"I shall have to think about it," he answered, polishing his riding boots with a tea-towel. "After all, even if I was still riding she's only going to be thirteen-two, rather small for me, don't you think?"

"I thought we were going to break her in together?" I said.

"I won't have the time, not in two years," he replied.

We heard a car stopping outside. Angus threw open the back door and rushed out. I heard him calling, "Yes, this is it. Drive into the yard. He's looking out of the second box . . ."

The woman who stepped out of a grey Lancia was called Lindsay Turtle. She had an upturned nose and was small and slim with grey eyes. I liked her at once.

"He looks nice enough," she said, studying Killarney. "What a lovely head. Why are you selling him? It's exams I suppose, the usual thing," she continued, looking at Angus.

"That's right. Shall I lead him out?" he asked.

He stood Killarney up and she felt his legs, while the sunlight danced on our cobbled yard. I thought, I hope she buys him and keeps him for ever, while Angus trotted him up and down the road.

We tacked him up together and Angus rode him in the paddock, sitting very straight in the saddle, trying to make a good impression.

"Where did you find him?" asked Lindsay Turtle.

"In Ireland. He belonged to a dealer called Donnie O'Reagan, a super man," I said. "We are his first real home. He's a horse in a million."

I was playing the part Angus wanted, not for him, but because I wanted Lindsay Turtle to buy Killarney, because she would be a good home. She mounted quickly while Angus held the other stirrup. She rode Killarney quietly and suddenly he *did* look a horse in a million—she was that sort of rider. She would have made the humblest horse look terrific.

"I hope she buys him," I told Angus.

"We are selling him too cheap," he answered. "We should have asked four thousand."

She cantered Killarney and he looked like a show hunter, with his head steady and his stride long and balanced.

"He's wasted on us," I said.

"On me, you mean," answered Angus.

"Can you put up a jump?" she called. "Anything will do."

We had a few heavy poles and some petrol cans, a couple of oil drums and an old door painted in different colours to look like a wall. We made a hog's-back, a triple, and put up the wall.

"That's lovely," she called.

Killarney danced a little. He cleared the hog's-back, did a cat jump over the wall and knocked down the triple.

"He hasn't jumped for some time," said Angus.

We put them up again and he jumped better this time. "He's very promising," she said. "What's he like in traffic?"

"Super, no trouble at all," answered Angus.

"Come on, he must have something wrong somewhere," she argued.

"No. He's always been perfect," said Angus.

"Is he for you?" I asked, because I had to know.

"If he's good enough. If not I shall sell him on to a nice teenager," she answered. "And I mean nice."

Angus looked at his watch, then he looked at me and smiled. "There's someone arriving to look at Killarney in ten minutes," he said. "I don't want to rush you. If you want to think about him, that's fine . . ."

"I think I want him. You said two thousand pounds didn't you? Can I give him a bit of a gallop?"

We took her along the road to where Dominic gallops his point-to-pointers down a long grass strip between plough. It goes up hill and down dale and it stretches for nearly a mile.

"I can promise you he's sound in wind and limb," announced Angus, looking at his watch again. "You can go as far as you like, it's clear all the way."

"Why are you in such a hurry?" I asked.

"It's good business."

"I feel as though I was selling a friend," I said.

"Don't be soppy," answered Angus.

"Why don't you go back and look for our next customer. He may have arrived by now."

I didn't move, because far away down the track

I could see Lindsay Turtle dismounting. "Look," I shouted, "something's gone wrong."

"Don't be silly. She's testing him. She'll get on in a minute, or she's dropped her whip."

"She wasn't carrying one," I answered.

We heard her shout something, then she picked up one of Killarney's forelegs and looked inside the hoof. Suddenly I remembered my prayer of the night before, and I couldn't look at Angus when he said in a horrified voice, "He must be lame. Oh no! How sickening—but why?" Then he was running down the track towards Killarney, calling, "He's never been lame before, I promise. What can have happened?"

I turned towards the yard, not knowing whether to cry or laugh, and feeling guilty at the same time.

I found a strange man knocking on the front door when I reached Sparrow Cottage and he said rather crossly, "Oh, there you are. Where's the horse?"

His son was with him, a smaller edition of the same person. They both wore checked caps, hacking jackets, breeches and boots.

"The horse is just returning, a lady has been trying him," I answered. "He may be sold. I'm not sure . . ."

"I see," said the father rather disagreeably. "In that case our journey will have been for nothing."

"You might have warned us," said the son, who spoke as though he had a marble in his mouth. "We are rather busy people."

"Here he is," I answered, and as I spoke I could hear Killarney's uneven hoofbeats on the road and knew he was still lame.

"Captain Hickman," said the man, holding out

his hand when he saw Angus. "And this is my son, George."

Angus had a hunted look on his face. He said, "I'm so sorry, but Killarney has just gone lame. It has never happened before."

"I'm afraid it was my fault. I was galloping him when it happened. He must be throwing a splint or something. I can't think of anything else. It's frightfully bad luck, I must say. But I'm still interested in the horse, when and if he's sound again," said Lindsay Turtle.

"Thank you very much," said Angus, taking Killarney's reins. "We'll ring the vet at once, and let you know when he's better."

Captain Hickman ran an expert hand down Killarney's forelegs while Lindsay Turtle drove away. "There's no heat anywhere. How extraordinary," he said. "It'll probably swell up later, though. No ill feelings. It's just bad luck."

"Thank you for taking it so well," said Angus. "And I'm sorry you've wasted your time."

"That's all right."

They were leaving now, talking to one another in low voices, no doubt trying to decide where to go next.

"Well," cried Angus, when the sound from their car had died away, "why did it happen? Why? He's never been lame before. Why today of all days?"

"Perhaps it was fate," I muttered. "Or God, or just bad luck, or like that woman said, he's throwing a splint."

"Horses throw splints when they're being worked hard. Killarney has hardly been ridden in the last three months. Don't make me laugh . . ."

23

He sounded furious and bitter at the same time, and he kept staring at me as though it was my fault.

"You wanted him to go lame, didn't you?" he accused me. "You willed it."

"I'm not a witch," I said. "But I am pleased because now he can't be sold, or not until he's sound. That may take weeks or months and by then you may have changed your mind." And I rushed into the house, slamming the door after me.

I walked up and down the kitchen, which had a Welsh dresser, a big table in the middle and checked curtains at the windows, and I wished that Mum was at home to calm Angus. I could hear him swearing in the yard and when he came indoors he ran upstairs, slammed his bedroom door and turned on his record-player so loud that my head started to ache.

I made myself some coffee and sat at the kitchen table. I thought, life goes on, the clock is still ticking the minutes away; all this will pass— Angus's anger, Killarney's lameness, and tomorrow will be a new day. But it didn't make me feel any better. I felt as if I was to blame for everything, for Killarney's lameness, for wasting everyone's time. Lindsay Turtle would have been a good home and Angus would have had his moped if I hadn't prayed, I thought. Then Angus opened his bedroom door and shouted, "Ring the vet, will you? It's the only thing we can do," then slammed the door again. I went to the telephone thinking, "Why me?"

Our vet was small and dark, with quick sensitive hands, and was called Mike Hunt. His receptionist answered the telephone and said that he would

24

visit us before nightfall if he had time. "But you know it's extra on Saturday's, don't you? Can it wait until Monday?" she asked.

I said, "Hold on," and shouted upstairs, "Can it wait until Monday, Angus?" but his music was so loud he couldn't hear.

"We would rather he made it today, please," I said, going back to the telephone. Suddenly I felt very tired. I put down the receiver and wandered outside. I looked at Killarney's leg, but there was nothing to see, and I thought, perhaps I'm a witch with supernatural powers. Perhaps if I pray, his leg will be better, but I didn't pray because the words wouldn't come. He and Phantom were grazing together, shoulder to shoulder, and they seemed to belong in the orchard. It is their home, I thought, just as the cottage is mine, and suddenly selling a horse seemed one of the saddest things in the world.

When I went back to the house, Mrs Parkin had arrived.

"What do you want for lunch, Jean?" she called. "It's twelve-thirty already and there's not a potato peeled."

"Anything. I don't care. Treacle tart, please, bacon, and scrambled eggs on toast." She looked plump and comforting. I nearly told her everything, but just as I was beginning, Angus came into the kitchen, crying, "How about a cup of tea, Mrs Parkin, and how are all your many children?" and the moment was gone.

3

Mike Hunt arrived later, when dusk had come to the yard, birds were chirping sleepily in their nests and the primroses had closed their petals.

He leapt out of the car calling, "Which one?" Killarney and Phantom were still coming in for the night and we had just put them to bed.

"The grey," answered Angus, fetching a head-collar. "He went lame this morning when someone was trying him and there's absolutely nothing to see."

"Whoa, old fellow," said Mike Hunt, slipping into the box after Angus, and running his hands down Killarney's forelegs. "Which one is it, then?" he asked.

Angus looked perplexed. "I can't remember. Which was it, Jean?" he asked.

I couldn't remember either, so we led him out and trotted him up the road. It was the off foreleg, and he wasn't any better.

"I can't understand it," said Mike Hunt. "There's nothing to see at all. I'll just get my hammer."

He tapped Killarney's hoof in every possible place, but Killarney didn't flinch. He stood, half angel, half horse, staring into the distance.

"Amazing," said Mike, putting his hammer away. "We can X-ray the leg if it gives any more trouble. In the meantime I'll give you some lotion to put on under a bandage.

Always in a hurry, he ran out to his car again, handed Angus a bottle, saying, "Soak a dressing in it and keep it on for at least twelve hours and ring me if he isn't better in a week, or if there's any new developments. If he gets worse, we'll have his shoe off." Then he slammed his car door and was gone.

"No comfort there," said Angus angrily. "Where's the gamgee? And what about the leg bandages?"

By the time we had finished bandaging Killarney's leg, the sky was full of stars.

"I shall never get the moped now," said Angus, leading the way indoors.

"He will get better; he must," I replied.

"The advertisement took all my spare cash," Angus answered.

We had just finished a supper of scrambled eggs on toast when the telephone rang. I answered.

"Geoff Craig," said a man's voice. "I saw your advertisement. Is the horse sold?" I looked at Angus, who was listening.

"No, he's not quite sound," I answered. "Otherwise he would be. We've had the vet and it is nothing serious. I'm sorry."

"That's all right, dear, we'll come anyway," said Geoff Craig. "Where are you?"

I gave him directions from the motorway. "Is he for you?" I asked.

"No, for my daughter—she competes, but we

27

can always wait for him to get sound again. We are not in any hurry," he said.

"That's fine then, see you tomorrow morning." I replaced the receiver slowly.

"You are a fool," shouted Angus. "Why did you say he wasn't sound?"

"Because I'm honest by nature."

"But he may be all right by tomorrow," said Angus.

"He didn't sound particularly nice," I told him. "Surely it would be better for him to go to Lindsay Turtle when he's sound."

"But I want the money by Monday."

"Damn the moped and damn Monday," I shouted. "You haven't got a heart, Angus. You don't care a damn where poor Killarney goes." I threw my dirty plate in the sink and rushed upstairs.

Later, Mum rang from Geneva, but she was in a hurry, so I didn't tell her about Killarney, only that we were still alive, and eating properly, cleaning our teeth, and locking up before going to bed. She rang off, and I returned to bed filled with a great sadness which weighed on me as heavily as a load of bricks.

It was raining the next morning. Angus was up first, grooming Killarney, taking off his bandage, praying that he was sound. I turned Phantom straight into the orchard.

"I shall never sell him," I told Angus. "He's my best friend and one doesn't sell friends."

"No one would buy him anyway, he's far too difficult," replied Angus, laughing.

The church bells were ringing across the fields,

telling us it was Sunday. Were they ringing in Geneva, too, I wondered?

"I suppose I had better clean his tack," said my brother, rolling up a bandage.

"Please yourself," I answered.

"Why don't you go out for a ride, or something?" asked Angus. "I don't need you."

"I want to see where Killarney goes, so that when I make my fortune I can buy him back," I answered.

"Great words," said my brother.

I felt too upset for breakfast. Angus trotted Killarney along the road and he was still lame. Rain began falling in torrents from the sky.

"I wish he would come," said Angus. "I want to clinch my deal over the moped."

We returned indoors and made coffee. The church bells had stopped ringing. "Are you going to cook a joint?" asked Angus. "There's one in the freezer."

"No, certainly not. We'll eat ham out of a tin," I answered disagreeably.

"I can see I need a girl-friend," said Angus. "My socks need darning and my jeans are split."

"Buy some new ones, then," I said, going upstairs to brush my hair—then changing my shirt, wishing that my nose was straighter, my brow higher, my legs thinner. Stupid Angus, I thought, he's like a child of ten. And he's a male chauvinist!

Soon after, a car turned into the yard and I rushed down to meet Geoff Craig and his daughter, who was called June. They were already looking at Killarney over his box door when I arrived, but Angus had the decency to say, "This is my sister, Jean." They turned to smile at me and

I saw that Geoff Craig had a bluff, unlined face with eyes too small for his plump cheeks and thick lips, and that June was wearing nail varnish and was slim with immaculate jodhs, long polished boots, a proper riding coat and gloves.

"Pleased to meet you," she said without enthusiasm.

"He looks a good sort," said Geoff Craig, alluding to Killarney. "What do you think, June?"

"Yes, not bad at all," she answered without much interest in her voice.

"Can we see him out," asked Geoff Craig.

"Yes, of course," said Angus.

They looked at Killarney for ages, and when June wasn't looking at Killarney I could see her sizing up Angus, and I soon decided that she liked what she saw.

"Shall I trot him up?" asked Angus.

"Not too far if he's lame, son," said Geoff Craig. "We just want to see his action. That's right, isn't it, June?"

"Sure," she said.

I thought of someone buying me a horse. I would be overcome with excitement, wildly enthusiastic. I looked at June and she was studying her nails.

"Have you many horses?" I asked.

"Only two or three," she said.

"Why do you want Killarney then?"

"To bring on," she said, looking at Angus again as though she was viewing him rather than Killarney.

"Well, what do you want to do—come again when he's sound?" he asked.

We were all wet now.

"Let's talk inside somewhere, shall we?" suggested Geoff Craig.

"Yes, of course, come indoors and have a drink," said Angus, sounding like Dad. "Jean, take them in. "

I led the way indoors. The cottage was in a bit of a muddle.

"What will you drink?" I asked, going to the cupboard.

Geoff Craig chose whisky, his daughter wanted a gin and orange. I went to the kitchen for ice. When I returned, Angus had arrived and was mixing the drinks. It was noon by this time and we all sat down and muttered "Cheers". Angus was drinking beer. I didn't drink anything.

"Well, it's like this," began Geoff Craig after a short silence. "I like the horse. He's just what we are looking for, but of course we haven't tried him, so we don't know how he goes, though I'm willing to take your word for it."

"He's super. I can guarantee that," said Angus.

"And then, of course, he is lame and we don't know why."

"Exactly," agreed Angus, swilling beer.

"And that is the second drawback."

"Yes, of course," replied Angus.

"I tell you what," said Geoff Craig, after rather a prolonged silence, when June stared solidly at Angus who turned red, "I'm willing to buy him at a price; it's a gamble, of course."

"Wouldn't you rather wait and have a vet's certificate?" I asked. "We want him to have a good home, that counts more than anything else."

"He'll have that all right," replied Geoff Craig.

"I can promise you that. June looks after her horses like babies, don't you, dear?"

She was studying her nails again, but she managed to say, "Yes, Dad."

I thought she's an imbecile, and imbeciles are not capable of looking after horses. "I think, it would be fairer to wait for a vet's certificate," I said.

Geoff Craig ignored me. He plunged his hands into his coat pocket and drew out a plastic bag. "There are nine hundred pounds here in cash," he said, "how about it?" as though he was bestowing a gift on us.

I said, "It's too little. He's worth more than that." But Angus was looking at the money and, as he looked, a cold shiver went down my spine and I thought, oh no, he's thinking of that moped and he's going to say 'yes'.

"Count it. Here, take it."

The money was in Angus's hands; large, twenty-pound notes, which Angus started to count.

"It is too little," I said again. "Killarney is cheap at a thousand pounds. Even two thousand is a give-away price. Nine hundred is absolutely ridiculous."

"But I don't usually buy lame horses, but we've come a long way and we've got the trailer outside. I don't want to go home empty-handed," explained Geoff Craig, helping himself to more whisky as though he owned the place.

Angus was still counting. He looked mesmerised. I said, "We can't sell at that price, Mr Craig," but he ignored me and June said, "He isn't your horse."

"He'll have a lovely home, I promise you that

he'll want for nothing. We spoil our horses. My wife treats them like children—carrots on Sunday, sugar at tea-time—you know what I mean, don't you?"

Angus suddenly smiled, as though he had just won a mental battle and was going to announce his decision.

I felt faint with fear. I put my head in my hands and waited.

"Have some more beer, Angus," said Geoff Craig. "Where's the bottle? And how is your glass, June? Here, let me top it up."

"We can't sell Killarney for that price," I said. "It's too little. It's total madness."

They continued talking as though I didn't exist, and now they were laughing and I heard Angus say, "Yes, that's all right if it's a good home. Take him, it'll save Dad the vet's bills . . ."

He put the money in his pocket and he didn't look at me. Then they all shook hands, and June nodded farewell to me with what I thought was triumph in her eyes. I looked at Angus and thought, "Judas".

I followed them to the stableyard. It wasn't raining any more and Killarney whinnied when he saw Angus, bringing tears to my eyes.

"You're going to a new home, old fellow," said Angus, putting on a headcollar. "Now be a good chap and always do your best. I want to see your name in the papers—'First, Killarney, ridden by Miss June Craig'." He smiled at June as he spoke and she smiled back.

Killarney followed Angus into the trailer, his wise eyes calm and trusting, while I stood numb with misery, suddenly speechless.

33

They tied him up. Angus threw up the ramp and they were still laughing. Then Geoff Craig turned to me and said, "Don't worry, Jean, he'll have the best home in the world, I promise you that."

Angus waved them into the road and Phantom started to gallop round the orchard, neighing in a demented manner. I started to cry. Then Killarney neighed from the trailer and it was like a last farewell and I started to scream at Angus. "How could you? How could you sell him to them?"

He raised his eyebrows and said, "I don't know what you mean." There was laughter behind the words, which made me feel like murder.

"We don't know them. You didn't even ask where they lived," I screamed.

"I shall get my moped tomorrow," said Angus, whistling. "You heard what they said—they are a good home. Better nine hundred in hand than two thousand in the bush."

It was like beating your head against a brick wall. Angus refused to understand. He wanted his conscience to be clear; he didn't want to feel guilty. He wanted his hands to feel clean.

Steam was rising from Phantom's back. I caught him, pushed him into his box and slammed the doors, top and bottom.

"He won't stay alone. I shall have to go down to the farm and get one of our ponies back to keep him company. I won't bother with lunch," I shouted after Angus's retreating figure.

I threw water on my tear-stained face and found two headcollars. The rain had stopped. Everything was glistening and the birds were singing again. A rainbow stretched across the horizon and the sky was suddenly clear and everything smelt of spring. I stared at Killarney's box and thought, he'll never look over the door again. Then I set off for the farm, thinking, in time I shall feel better, and when I see Killarney's name in the paper, I shall be able to say, "He used to be ours." But it didn't help.

4

Dominic's farm lay in a valley. The house was
built of brick and flint and there was a garden in
the front with a wall round it where straight rows
of vegetables grew. There was a large porch full
of wellington boots, and over everything hung the
soothing smell of cow. Mr Barnes was large and
weatherbeaten, with ruddy cheeks and grey hair.
Mrs Barnes was tiny, and rushed hither and
thither, rather like a hen scratching for worms.
Dominic was somewhere between the two, with
fair hair and blue-grey eyes. He was five foot eight
and immensely strong. I had known him and his
parents nearly all my life, and they had become as
familiar as the landscape. In fact, until today, I
had never really thought about them, they were
just there, like a tree or a hill.

I banged on the front door knocker while a cat
purred round my legs and a dog barked. Mrs
Barnes opened the door. "Oh, hallo, Jean," she
said. "Come in."

"I won't, if you don't mind. Is Dominic
around?" I asked.

The house smelt of Sunday lunch and though I
wasn't hungry, or thought I wasn't, my mouth
started to water. Mrs Barnes was wearing a pinny

and bedroom slippers. She wore her hair in a plait round her head.

"Dominic, it's Jean from the cottage," she called.

His boots were in the porch, and he was in his socks, a thick pullover and corduroy trousers.

"Hallo, Jean," he said. (He was one of those people who always say your name.)

"I wondered if I could take one of the ponies home," I asked. "Killarney's gone." And though I was trying to be sensible, there was a croak in my voice.

"Gone?" asked Dominic, putting on his boots.

"Sold."

"That's a shame," he said. "Which pony do you want to take?"

"Well, not Mermaid because your cousin rides her, doesn't she?" I asked.

"Yes, she does. But she *is* your pony, Jean," he answered.

"So I suppose Moonlight and Twilight."

"Tell you what," said Dominic, leading the way to the ponies' field. "Why not separate them? It's time they were parted. Why, Twilight is more than a year now, isn't he? I'll come with you, Jean, to make it easier and then I'll bring back Moonlight. How about it?"

"But what about your lunch?" I asked.

"That can keep," he answered, and started to call the ponies.

Mermaid was small and dappled grey, like a rocking-horse. Moonlight, Angus's old pony, was a lighter roany grey and bigger. Twilight, her foal, was pinky roan with a dear little star on her forehead.

37

"Here, you take Twilight and I'll go first with Moonlight," said Dominic. "It's a nice day for a walk."

The Barneses are always busy and yet somehow they always have time to help anyone in trouble. Time and time again they have come to our rescue, towing our car with a tractor, delivering hay in a snowstorm, looking after our ponies when we've been away. Dad calls them the salt of the earth.

We led the ponies across the fields to Sparrow Cottage and, as we walked, we talked.

"I'm sorry Killarney's gone, Jean," said Dominic. "Who bought him?"

"A man called Geoff Craig. His daughter hopes to win some events on him I think. I didn't like them much." And my stupid voice came out shaky, because I was still upset and near to tears. "I hate discussing it," I said. "I don't want it mentioned."

"Did you say Geoff Craig?" asked Dominic.

"Yes," I shouted, trying to walk ahead because I was crying again.

"How come?"

"What do you mean, how come?" I asked.

"Well, he trades in horse meat," said Dominic.

I stopped in my tracks and now it was my turn to say, "What do you mean?" while hammers seemed to be pounding in my head and every bit of me wanted to cry, "It isn't true!"

"He's always at the market. He buys up half the horses every month. He's got the horse meat business buttoned up. He ships the meat to Europe. The Shetlands go to Holland because they like little ponies for their sausages; the others go to France and Belgium. Didn't you know, Jean?" asked Dominic.

"No." I felt quite speechless and now I was shivering. "But he brought his daughter with him," I said, after a short silence.

"Oh, everyone knows her—June, isn't it? The biggest tart in town. Mind you, she can ride, Jean. She's won quite a lot. She keeps her horses a little way from those condemned to die. By the way, what made Angus sell Killarney in the first place?"

"It's a long story. He wants a moped," I replied miserably, sick with anguish.

"I could have let him have one, Jean. I've got one in a shed at the back of the house. I'm sick of the darned thing," said Dominic.

I remembered Killarney leaving; the way he had looked at Angus and trusted him. And Angus had betrayed that trust.

"What are we going to do?" I asked. "Are you sure he will go for meat?"

"Yes, Jean, because June has several horses already—she wouldn't want another. I would have bought Killarney if you had offered him to me. I had no idea he was for sale. How much did you get?"

I was ashamed to tell him. "Nine hundred miserable pounds," I answered. "To little, far too little. I told Angus so, but he had the money in his hands, lots of miserable, grubby twenty-pound notes."

"Has Angus gone mad, Jean?" asked Dominic.

"I don't know. Our parents are away. I thought we were going to have a lovely time riding, but it's been awful, horrible . . ."

We reached our cottage. Phantom was still pounding round his box. I opened the top door, and, seeing Moonlight and Twilight, he neighed.

"I'll put him out in the orchard," I said.

We put Moonlight in Killarney's old box and turned the other two out. They pounded round the orchard like mustangs, Twilight tiny with a sweet stumpy tail, Phantom gleaming gold and silver, more beautiful than any other horse I had ever known. Moonlight ate hay, unperturbed.

"I think she's glad to be rid of him. He's an awful tease," said Dominic, looking at Twilight with affection.

"Well, I must be going now, Jean," he said, a minute later.

"Not yet, not until we've decided something. We can't let Killarney go for meat," I cried.

"Do you want to buy him back, then?" asked Dominic.

"Yes, definitely," I cried.

Dominic said, "I'll tell you what we will do then, Jean. I'll borrow the Land Rover and we'll go to the abattoir first thing, and we'll wait for him to come in."

"And then . . . ?" I asked.

"We'll say he was bought under false pretences and make one hell of a row," said Dominic.

"Do you think it will work?"

"It will have to, won't it, Jean? It's lucky you sold him on a Sunday, or he might be dead already. Geoff Craig only keeps the thin ones, he fattens them, but Killarney has plenty of flesh on him," said Dominic.

"Where is the abattoir?" I asked.

"Fifty miles from here, and it opens early, so you had better be up at six," replied Dominic.

"We'll pay for the petrol."

"We'll talk about that later." Dominic was leading Moonlight away.

"Will you hoot or something?" I asked.

"Yes, at the gate. Be ready. And eat some breakfast—abattoirs are sickening places at the best of times," answered Dominic. "And don't forget the money."

I walked indoors, longing for the comforting presence of our parents, who would have known what to do, who could manage Angus.

"Killarney's gone for meat," I cried, my voice still shaky with emotion. "Did you hear—for meat?"

He was watching television with a plate of sausages and chips on his knees.

"How do you know?" he asked, suddenly pale, his eyes dazzled by the light I had switched on.

"Yes," I screamed. "While you sit there watching that stupid film, Killarney could be being skinned, only it's Sunday . . ."

"But how do you know?" asked Angus, following me into the kitchen. And suddenly I felt weary with emotion and an awful nagging sense of guilt.

"Because Geoff Craig deals in horse meat," I said.

"And June?"

"What does June matter?" I shouted. "She keeps her horses just a little separate and I dare say if they don't win enough or have the misfortune to go lame, they go for meat too. She's hard, can't you see? She has to be, or she couldn't stand it, could she?" I cried.

"Who told you this?"

"Dominic, and he's taking us to the abattoir tomorrow at six. He knows where it is. He knows everything. I feel such a fool by comparison," I

41

cried. "And *he'll* buy Killarney, I think, *and* he's got a moped for you . . ."

Angus then fell into a chair and hid his face, and I knew he was crying. I had not seen Angus cry for years and I didn't know what to say. After a time he started to wail, "I thought they were all right. I thought June was nice. I thought he would have a good home. How could they lie like that? The filthy swines, how could they?"

I put the kettle on while he continued moaning and crying, "God, how I hate myself, I'll never touch that filthy money as long as I live. It's like poison now. I'm going to wash my hands, they feel contaminated by it . . ."

He disappeared upstairs while I made myself a sandwich. The day seemed to have lasted for years already, though it was only half-past three. I wished it was tomorrow now, that we were already travelling to the abattoir in the Barnes's battered green Land Rover. The night will be agony, I thought, and what shall we do with the rest of the day, with this hanging over us? I knew that there was nothing worse in the world than waiting, waiting for another day to dawn before we could solve our problem, not knowing whether we would succeed.

Later our parents rang us.

"Don't tell them anything," cried Angus. "Please."

So I said that everything was all right and that we were eating lots of food and that Mrs Parkin was super. Afterwards, when they had rung off, Angus said, "Thank you. I don't want to worry them. It would be different if they could do anything, but they can't."

I decided to leave Phantom out for the night as spring had really come at last, and we spent the rest of the evening watching television. But I didn't really see it for I kept imagining Killarney's grey body hanging in an abattoir while men in blood-stained coats sharpened knives and hatchets to turn it into meat for the French. Then tears blinded my vision.

I don't think Angus took much in either, for he sat with his hands clasped together so tight that the knuckles showed white, and at every noise he jumped like a nervous horse in a strange field. At ten o'clock we decided to go to bed.

"I shan't sleep," said Angus. "I shall never sleep as long as Killarney's with Geoff Craig."

I nearly said, "And when he's dead, will you sleep then?"

We set our clocks for half-past five and crawled into our beds, sick with guilt and sadness.

For a time I lay there, waiting for sleep to come, but I could see nothing but Killarney dying in terrifying circumstances. Finally, I knelt on my bedside mat and prayed: "Please, God, save Killarney. Please let us have him back safe and sound."

Then I climbed into bed again and my room was full of moonlight, and I thought that Dominic Barnes was one of the nicest people I'd ever met, and if anyone could save Killarney he could, but it didn't help. Anxiety gnawed at my stomach and I thought of Mum coming back and listening to our sad tale, and Dad threatening to sue Geoff Craig for false pretences. Then I thought, if I hadn't made Killarney lame by my prayers he would be with Lindsay Turtle now, and so it's all my fault—and then, at last, I slept.

5

I wakened to my alarm clock and to the sound of birds singing fit to burst their lungs. Daylight streamed through my curtains while in the orchard Twilight neighed for his mother. I leapt from bed and rushed to Angus's room.

"It's time to get up. We're going to the abattoir," I shouted, beating on his door with my fists. I was glad to have the night behind me, to be setting out to save Killarney, for while there's life there's hope as doctors say.

"Go away. I'm awake," said Angus. 'It's only half-past five."

I dressed in jeans, a checked shirt and a blue sweater. I rushed downstairs and put the kettle on to boil. Oh, for time to pass, I thought, to be nearly there. Why does time pass so slowly when you want it to pass quickly, and when you want to linger because you're happy, it passes in a flash? It isn't fair, I felt, boiling myself an egg.

The sky outside was still rosy with the light of dawn. It was a day for hope, not despair, and it affected me. Everything seemed better this morning, more hopeful. It was as though salvation lay at hand.

"Why do you always get up half an hour earlier

than necessary?" asked Angus, appearing in the kitchen. "I wouldn't mind so much if you left me asleep, but you never do."

He looked more hopeful too. His face had lost its anguish.

"Have you got any money?" he asked next.

"Only fifty pence."

"We had better rob the housekeeping then," he replied.

"Remember to bring all those grubby notes," I said.

"I'm not an imbecile. And what if the abattoir men are paying a lot more?"

I hadn't thought of that. "Dominic will think of something," I said, after a moment.

"You talk of him as though he was God," replied Angus.

"At least he helps and cares about us," I answered. "If you ask me, he's our one and only friend."

"Your friend," said Angus.

"You don't like him, do you?" I asked.

"Not much; he lacks education."

I wanted to say all sorts of things but I didn't. The day was too lovely for argument and our errand too desperate. I went upstairs and helped myself to ten pounds out of the money Mum had left locked in a cupboard. Then I ate breakfast, washed up, tidied the kitchen, and it was still only five minutes to six.

"Let's lock up and wait outside," I suggested, to which Angus agreed.

Phantom and Twilight were still close to one another. An energetic man was running down our

lane in a track suit. The sky was blue, patterned
with small floating clouds.

"Here he is," said Angus.

Dominic stopped the Land Rover. "Hop in, "
he said.

He was wearing a checked cap. He looked like
a sporting farmer and older than his seventeen
years.

"I'm afraid she makes rather a noise," he said,
referring to the Land Rover. "She's not as young
as she was."

Angus grunted in reply.

"We had Mike Hunt out in the night to a calving
cow. He said that your horse was lame on
Saturday—was he really sound by Sunday?"

"No." I said.

"I don't suppose you'll ever understand how
horribly plausible Geoff Craig was," said Angus.
"He even told lies while he was drinking Dad's
whisky. He took me in all the way, so did June.
I thought she was shy but I suppose she was just
hideously embarrassed."

"I expect she earned a fiver for helping," said
Dominic. "She never does anything for nothing."

"Is Moonlight all right?" I asked.

"Yes, fine. Have you brought the money?"
Angus nodded.

"What if Killarney doesn't turn up?" I asked.

"We'll have to think again."

We passed through a town and then on to a
motorway where lorries belched fumes and angry
businessmen hooted at slower drivers.

"Peace, perfect peace, with dear ones far away,"
said Angus, to no one in particular.

"I know Geoff Craig," said Dominic presently.

"I see him in the market every time there's a horse sale and I always want to bash his head in. He buys all the sweet little ponies, and the old ones with years of work behind them who deserve a holiday before they die. He even buys mares and foals sometimes, and they say he buys stolen horses too, though no one has caught him yet—and he's made a fortune. He drives a Mercedes. He makes me want to vomit. Those pink cheeks should be turned black and blue, that's my opinion, anyway. What do you think, Jean?"

"I think he should be murdered, and the sooner the better," I replied.

It was now seven o'clock. Dominic looked at his watch and said, "The abattoir opens early. I'm not sure of the exact time, but I think it's soon after seven-thirty."

"And how many more miles is it?" asked Angus.

"About twenty."

We left the motorway. Dominic drove deftly as though born to it.

"This road tends to be a bit slow, it's all corners," he said. "Luckily it doesn't go on for long."

Angus sat silently, his hands knotted together. At times I thought he was praying. Then we left the twisty road and entered a town. We crossed a river and travelled through miles of neat suburbs, where dustbins stood on pavements, waiting to be collected.

"Not much further now," said Dominic.

And suddenly I knew I was frightened, frightened of not finding Killarney, of being too late, or simply of failing. At the same moment Dominic swore and pulled into the side of the road.

"No petrol," he said. "The pump must have packed up."

He jumped out of the Land Rover and threw up the bonnet. Sunlight danced on the windscreen. Qn each side, the gardens were full of crocuses and blossoming shrubs.

"Is it fatal?" I asked, getting out. "Shall we ever make it . . . ?"

"Sure, it's packed up before. I'll get it going," said Dominic, fetching a spanner from a box under the front seat.

"Shall I go to a garage?" asked Angus.

"Hang on."

But for how long? I thought.

"Try switching her on, now press the starter." Angus was in the driver's seat, but she wouldn't start.

"Could we walk and catch a bus?" I asked.

"Please shut up. I'm doing my best," said Dominic. His cap was in the road; his hands covered with oil.

"What about pushing it?" asked Angus.

"She hasn't got a flat battery, so pushing won't help," cried Dominic in an exasperated voice.

"We must keep quiet," said Angus as though *he* hadn't spoken.

Two children ran past us, laughing. People locked their front doors and set off for work. My heart was pounding against my ribs. I wanted to run on ahead—to do something—to be of some use.

"Try the starter again, Angus," said Dominic.

The engine groaned and died.

"I'm going to walk, catch a bus, hitch. Where is the abattoir? What's the address?" I cried.

"And what will you do there all by yourself, Jean?" asked Dominic with a smile behind his eyes. "Do you think you're a match for that lot?"

"It will be better than doing nothing, than standing here until it's too late," I answered. "He could be going in now. They could be killing him now, at this very moment. Can't we hire a car or call a garage? I've got ten pounds."

Dominic ignored me. His face looked shut. He was concentrating on one thing—getting the Land Rover going. Angus passed him tools, neither of them spoke.

"OK, try again," said Dominic. "Go on, keep trying."

Now we could all hear the petrol pump ticking; Angus revved up the engine. Dominic and I leapt in; then we were moving again, racing through the flowery suburb, ignoring the speed limit.

"We'll soon be there," said Dominic, turning to smile at me. "And we won't be too late. I bet you my best boots that Geoff Craig never rises before eight!"

We left the suburbs behind and drove along a road lined with factories. We passed an old car dump, a collection of gipsy caravans, and a tethered donkey.

Then we reached another town, turned left towards a murky river and stopped.

"Is this it?" asked Angus.

"Just about, just round the corner. Has anybody got any questions or ideas?" asked Dominic.

"Nothing much," said Angus.

"We just rush in then, like the Charge of the Light Brigade?" suggested Dominic, starting the engine again.

We drove across concrete to a wide open space. I saw big corrugated iron doors, a horse box, men arguing. I looked at Dominic and said, "Are we in time?"

"Are you sure this is the right place? There's no notice or anything," said Angus.

"There is a notice somewhere, it says it's regularly inspected which I bet it isn't."

Dominic was on the ground, looking about him. I felt frozen to my seat, unable to move. There was no Killarney, no horse to be seen, just arguing men and a bright April day, with the sun shining over the murky river. From the tall factory chimneys beyond it came a smell of gas.

Dominic went across to the men. He had left his cap behind in the road. I watched them talking. Then he came back.

"They are on strike," he cried, beginning to laugh. "They aren't killing anything today, or tomorrow. They have put in a claim for twenty pounds more a week and the management won't pay it."

"Aren't there other abattoirs?" asked Angus after a moment.

"They are *all* on strike," cried Dominic, laughing. "The whole blooming lot."

He climbed into the Land Rover again.

"We should have listened to the seven o'clock news; I usually do. It might have saved us a journey," he said, still laughing. "Can't you see? We've got two days at least now. We've got time to make a plan, to save Killarney and who knows what else . . ."

He turned the Land Rover. I looked for piles of hooves, för rotting skulls, but there was nothing.

The abattoir was quite near civilisation but it seemed that no one knew or cared. Why don't people parade with placards saying 'stop the killing of horses for meat now'? I wondered. Why doesn't someone do something?

"People say we eat cattle, so why not horses?" said Dominic, as though he had read my thoughts.

"But you don't ride cattle, persuade them to trust you, share your life with them. You don't love them or tell them you're their friend."

"Exactly," agreed Angus. "But what do we do next?"

"Make a plan—did Geoff Craig tell you where he lived?" asked Dominic.

Angus shook his head.

"Well, Dad will know," said Dominic.

We had reached the suburbs again. We seemed to be travelling much faster than before. Dominic stopped to fill up with petrol and I handed him the ten-pound note. He handed it back again.

"Don't be silly," said Angus. "You must take it."

"But I'm going to do well out of it," answered Dominic. "Because I want to buy Killarney for nine hundred pounds. I want to hunt and ride him in point-to-points. Dad's old chaser is really past it and I've always envied you Killarney. I'm not doing this for love, you know, though Jean can ride him in the Ladies Race if she likes. I want the horse."

Angus looked a little askance at this.

"And you can have my moped thrown in for nothing," Dominic added. "I hate the thing. I'd rather have a horse any day."

"Nothing is that simple," replied Angus.

"Well, it is for me. Perhaps being a farmer brings one down to earth. I see black and white, not grey."

Soon we were back on the motorway and it was nine o'clock.

"Call and ride my horses any time, Jean," Dominic said. "They don't get enough exercise. And you too, Angus, if you can spare the time.

We thanked him and fell silent.

Ten minutes later, Dominic dropped us at the cottage.

"Why don't you come down to my place this evening? Mum will give you a spot of tea and then we can make a plan afterwards. Say after milking, about six—how's that?" he asked.

"Super," I replied, before Angus had time to speak.

"Six o'clock then."

We watched him drive away.

"He's arrogant," said Angus.

"But kind," I answered.

"I don't know whether to let him have Killarney or not, because I want him back now. It's just that after exams I want to go abroad for a bit," Angus said.

"But we haven't got him back yet," I answered. "We may never get him back. Geoff Craig may refuse to sell. Haven't you thought of that?"

"Of course I have," said Angus.

When we went inside we found Mrs Parkin cleaning the cottage, so I decided to school Phantom in the paddock. He still wasn't stopping straight and his canter lacked cadence.

Angus rang up the people who were keeping the

moped for him. "I can't buy it," he said. "I'm so sorry." But he didn't sound sorry.

I ate bread and cheese washed down with tea before catching Phantom. The day still felt full of hope, and everywhere plants were breaking into bud, the leaves were new and green on the trees, and the grass was pushing through the mud of winter, thin and weak but still there.

Phantom liked work. He would be a good circus horse. He learned very quickly, but this also had disadvantages, for he was capable of learning a dressage test in no time at all, and then he anticipated everything and his movements became abrupt and jerky instead of calm and balanced.

When I had finished schooling it was lunch-time. Mrs Parkin had made steak and kidney pie, and rhubarb crumble.

"I can see you haven't been eating properly. You look terrible," she said.

"Thank you very much, but it's something else which makes us look terrible," replied Angus.

After lunch he showed me a piece of paper on which was written:

SAVING KILLARNEY. Suggestions.
1. Offer to buy him back—this is unlikely to succeed.
2. Sue for false pretences. This will take too long.
3. Steal. This is unlawful.

"So you see, there's nothing we can do," he said mournfully, when I had read it. "We have absolutely no basis for getting Killarney back."

"We must keep thinking. Dominic may have an idea," I answered.

"Soon the abattoirs will be open again; time is

running out. Did you read the paper this morning? The workers' union is meeting the management on Wednesday. They could be back to work by Thursday," Angus answered.

"That still gives us two days," I replied. "A lot can happen in two days."

"For us or against, that is the question," replied Angus. "I'm going to ring inquiries anyway," he said, going to the telephone. "I want to talk to Geoff Craig. I want to tell him what I think of him."

"Don't be rude," I said. "Be polite, say we will buy him back—pay a bit more. Offer him a thousand.

"I haven't got a thousand," replied Angus, dialling.

"We'll raise it somehow," I answered.

The girl at inquiries was not very helpful. She said, "Town please."

Angus only knew the county. Then she asked "Initial?"

Angus answered, "G," and we both knew it could be his second christian name.

"There are thirty-five Craigs in the county and not one of them has G as an initial. Do you want me to look further?" asked the girl in an exasperated voice after less than a minute.

"No, thank you," replied Angus, replacing the receiver.

"Dominic may know," I said.

"I don't want to ask him for help. I'm sick of asking him. I'm not six years old," cried Angus.

"But Geoff Craig may be ex-directory," I suggested.

"If he had written a cheque we would know his

real initial," replied Angus, pacing up and down the kitchen.

"And we might have been able to trace him through his bank," I said.

"How I hate the word if—if, if, if—and all the while time is passing," cried Angus. "Do you realise that we will never have today again?"

"I don't want it again, not one minute of it," I answered. "I wish it was over. I wish our parents were home and Killarney back in his stable. I wish the last few days had never happened."

Angus was looking through the Yellow Pages telephone directory. His hair was on end and he hadn't washed his face since yesterday.

He was looking under 'HORSE DEALERS', muttering "Craig" to himself.

"Shall I ring Dominic?" I asked. "Because it's our only hope. He knows the address, or his father does."

"He knows everything, doesn't he?" replied Angus. "I will ring him myself. I just hoped to get by without him for once."

We drank some coffee to raise our spirits and then Angus dialled the number we both knew by heart. It was a long time before anyone answered and all the time I could feel my heart pounding against my side. At last Angus said, "Dominic? It's Angus." He explained what he wanted.

Dominic answered, "Hang on, I'll get it. The number is under 'FARMERS' . . ."

Two minutes later Angus was dialling another number, holding the receiver as though it was a weapon, as though it held the only hope left. He said, "This is Angus Simpson speaking. Is that Mr Craig? I sold you a grey horse over the weekend.

Yes, a grey called Killarney; well, I want to buy him back." His voice was tense, and crackly with emotion. "I am willing to pay extra, to make it worth your while."

I guessed that Dominic had told him what to say. I was biting my knuckles as I waited for Angus to smile, to say, "Thank you".

Instead, he shifted his weight from one foot to the other and said, "I see. Do you really mean that? I don't want him to go for meat. He's a wonderful horse, kind and generous. He'll jump anything across country. I am willing to give you another two hundred. I should never have sold him. I regret it deeply. Please let me buy him back."

I could hear Geoff Craig shouting, "When I buy a horse I don't sell him back a few days later. I keep him. Is that clear? Don't bother me again. No is my final word on the subject. He's my daughter's now. We made a deal and that's the end of it." Then he slammed down his receiver, while Angus seemed to turn a shade whiter.

"He's insane," I said.

Angus was dialing Dominic's number.

"It's no good," he shouted into the receiver. "He won't sell him back to us, not even with an extra two hundred. He still pretends he's for June, but I know by his voice that it isn't true. He's just a liar. I don't know what we can do now.

Dominic said, "Come over right away. Don't waste another minute. And don't despair. We'll make a plan. There's still time."

6

Mrs Barnes opened the farmhouse door for us.

"Come right in," she said. "Don't mind your shoes. We don't worry about a bit of mud."

Inside, the house was low-ceilinged. Coats hung in a narrow hall. Tea was already laid in the large kitchen where there were comfortable chairs as well as stiff-backed ones.

"Dominic is still milking. He will be in in a minute," she said. "Sit yourselves down."

We had changed into tidy clothes. I sat down and a cat jumped on my knee. There were framed photographs of horses on the walls, which Angus started to study.

Then Dominic came in. "Hallo, I'm just going to wash," he said, while his mother started to make the tea.

Suddenly it all seemed irrelevant to me. Here we were, preparing to eat while Killarney was under sentence of death, and the ancient clock on the old-fashioned chimney-piece was ticking away the minutes to his execution.

There was cold beef on the table, pickles, chutney, two home-made cakes, bread and butter, cheese, fruit. High tea at its very best. Mr Barnes hung up his coat before he sat down. Underneath, he wore braces over a striped shirt; old trousers, boots. His stomach hung over the top of his trousers.

We talked about the weather and Dominic looked embarrassed, half ashamed and half proud of his parents. Angus and I ate like wolves, encouraged by Mrs Barnes. The evening sun barely filtered through the small windows.

"Do you think you'll get him back?" said Mr Barnes suddenly, cutting himself some cheese. "The horse, I mean," he added, after a short uncertain silence.

"I don't know," answered Angus.

"We hope so," I said, at the same moment.

"He should go to prison," said Mr Barnes.

We finished our pieces of cake and drained our cups of tea.

"That's where he should be. Horses were never meant for eating, or only when men are starving. And there's plenty of beef about—too much," said Mr Barnes.

Dominic stood up. "Let's discuss strategy in my room," he suggested.

"What about the washing-up?" I asked, carrying my plates and teacup to the sink.

"Leave it, Jean. Forget it," said Mrs Barnes.

"You don't want to listen to Dad," said Dominic, leading the way up narrow stairs. His room looked towards the cows houses and milking parlour. It had brown linoleum on the floor and sporting prints on the walls. It was a cold, bare room. Dominic switched on a heater.

"Now for a plan," he said.

"We must be quick. Time is running out," replied Angus, in a tight voice.

"I have a plan. I thought of it in the middle of the night. I don't think Jean is going to like it, though," said Dominic.

"What do you mean?" I asked.

"It concerns Phantom, and you know how you are about him," replied Dominic, with a faint smile.

I was sitting on his bed, which had an old-fashioned white bedspread on it. I felt suddenly afraid.

"Well, spell it out," I cried.

"But it's got nothing to do with Phantom," said Angus.

"We need proof," continued Dominic, sitting on a small white chair.

"What proof?" interrupted Angus impatiently.

"Proof that he bought Killarney on false pretences. For that we must sell him another horse. And I will be the witness."

"Not Phantom," I cried.

"We'll get him back," said Dominic. "I want him to say his piece. I am going to sell him Phantom as a stolen horse."

"And I am going to tape it all," cried Angus, suddenly coming to life. "My tape-recorder is tiny . . . and it's almost soundless . . ."

"He'll know us," I gasped, frantically trying to think of objections.

"Perfect," cried Dominic, leaping to his feet to pace the room.

"We'll change our appearance. Angus, you can wear a moustache," said Dominic, beginning to laugh. "And you can be my wife, Jean. We'll get you a wig."

"Very funny," I answered, not knowing whether

to laugh or cry, and with a sinking feeling in my stomach.

"I belong to the local drama group. We can hire the things," said Dominic. "We'll go tomorrow after milking. That's Tuesday, and on Wednesday we'll sell him Phantom."

"We won't have *any* horses then," I said. "And supposing we can't get either of them back? I can't bear it."

"Don't blubber," said Angus.

"I don't want to be your wife, Dominic."

"Girl-friend, then. It doesn't matter. You can wear a headscarf if you don't like a wig. We'll make you up, so he won't know you. You can be very quiet—a bit dim. And you can smoke. I'll get some cigarettes."

"She'll keep coughing," said Angus.

"Shut up; it's all your fault," I answered.

"We'll have to rehearse," continued Dominic, as though neither of us had spoken. "Phantom will be mine and stolen, I'll make that clear. Angus, you can be my mate and you must do the recording. Jean, you're just another witness."

"Thank you very much," I answered.

"I'm in a hurry to get rid of Phantom, so I will accept a few hundred, that should whet his appetite," said Dominic. "Oh, I'm looking forward to it. And you can disappear for the police when we have the recording, Angus, because we want to take Phantom and Killarney back with us—right?"

"Right," agreed Angus.

"I don't know whether I can bear it," I said slowly.

"You must, it's for the good of the whole horse world," replied Dominic. "We are going to expose

Geoff Craig and his darling daughter for what they are."

"And to retrieve Killarney," added Angus, standing up, preparing to leave.

"I'll arrange for us to get the clothes we need. Let's meet here at eleven tomorrow," suggested Dominic, following us downstairs.

"OK," said Angus.

"I'll clean out the trailer; at the moment it's full of pig's muck," said Dominic.

"I wish we could go there tomorrow," I exclaimed. "I can't bear waiting a minute longer."

"We need time to think. We can't afford to make a mistake," replied Dominic.

"You know the abattoirs may be open on Thursday, don't you?" I asked.

"Yes, but we'll be there by eleven on Wednesday morning. If that fails, we'll get an injunction to stop them killing Killarney, but that won't be easy," replied Dominic.

Dusk had come when we started to walk home. I felt very alone at this moment. I wanted to scream—you are risking Phantom and he's my horse and you haven't even asked. But it seemed pointless, for now there was no other way to save Killarney.

We ran down the lane which leads to the farm, then along the footpath which leads home. Neither of us spoke. I imagined Phantom going, Dominic accepting cash, dirty notes in a plastic bag. I shall have to wear dark glasses, I thought, or Geoff Craig will notice that I'm crying.

The trees were full of chirping birds. Our cottage looked asleep, the chequered slopes on each side like a patchwork eiderdown. I longed for someone to be there to welcome us, but of course it was empty. Angus put the kettle on.

"You are very silent," he said. "But I promise you we'll get Phantom back again."

"But he will have been sold, can't you see?" I cried. "And supposing Geoff Craig doesn't say anything incriminating? What then?"

"Dominic will handle it. He's no fool."

"He may make a mistake," I answered. "He may let us down, miscalculate, misjudge; no one is always right."

"We'll have to risk that," said Angus.

"We can't lose both horses. What will our parents say? Oh, I feel ill," I cried, "ill to the marrow, sick with fear. I can't live without Phantom. I can't even endure school without him. Can't you understand?"

"Only half," replied Angus, pouring hot water on to tea-leaves.

"He's my escape. When school has been awful I ride him into the woods and everything is all right again," I said. "Without him I shall be lost. What shall I do all day? How shall I fill up my time? I'll go mad."

"We'll get him back. Both of them will be here, grazing under the apple trees just as they used to. We'll bring them back on Wednesday, I promise," replied Angus.

"If only I could believe you. You're asking so much," I said. "You're asking me to sell my horse to save yours."

"Not just mine, other people's too, to expose the whole racket."

"But selling horses for meat isn't illegal," I answered.

"But promising them a good home and every care, and then having them killed is," replied Angus.

"Are you sure?"

"Yes."

But I couldn't be sure. I wanted the law in front of me, written down, not Angus's and Dominic's assumptions. I looked out into the darkness and I didn't trust anyone any more.

The next day Dominic drove us to a store of theatrical clothes. It was above a brewery in a building which dated back to Elizabethan times. He chose himself a faded homburg hat and Angus tried on moustaches, and in spite of what lay ahead, we couldn't help laughing.

We tried on wigs and I became a redhead with a patterned scarf tied under my chin. I looked awful, quite different, years older.

Angus chose a moustache which turned down at the ends. It changed him completely. He found a checked waistcoat and a lumber jacket. Dominic only wanted the hat. We paid on the way out and promised to bring everything back before the weekend.

I rode after lunch, and each moment was sacred because I might never ride Phantom again. He was full of energy, glad to be out, but searching for something, too, stopping to stare into the distance, to neigh and paw the ground whenever we halted. I decided that he was looking for Killarney and I patted his neck. "Don't worry, tomorrow you'll be together again," I told him. And the words made me believe it.

We had a last gallop down the track to

Dominic's farm and back, and Phantom seemed to go faster than ever before, or maybe it was just my imagination.

When I returned home, Angus was self-consciously cleaning Killarney's tack. "I want it ready for him," he said. He had bedded down his box as well and hung a full hay net near the door.

I turned Phantom out with Twilight in the orchard, and watched him roll, and another day was nearly gone. Now I was counting the hours until everything was over and we were home again with our two horses grazing together under the trees.

I started to clean my tack. It was old and comfortable; the bit and stirrups were stainless steel and the girth was folded leather.

"Dominic is going to be here at eight-thirty to box Phantom. He says not to bandage, etc. Don't groom him, either. He must look as though he's been stolen out of a field—and we're to use our oldest headcollar, the one tied together with string."

"He rang up, then?" I asked, the sinking feeling in my stomach worse than ever.

"Yes. And he's painted the farm trailer a different colour so it won't be noticed. He won't accept any thanks," replied Angus.

"What else did he say?"

"To have a good breakfast because an army can't march on an empty stomach, and if you faint your wig might fall off."

"Very funny," I answered. "If Phantom goes for meat I shall kill myself, did you tell him that?"

"No."

I finished cleaning my tack and wandered

indoors. I put the television on, but nothing seemed to register. I picked up a book but the words were just a jumble in front of my eyes. I looked at the time and it was five o'clock. The day seemed to have lasted for eternity already.

Mrs Parkin had brought us a cake. She had cleaned the whole cottage from top to bottom and the garden was full of washing put out to dry. The desk in the sitting-room was covered with schedules of shows in which I had intended to compete, but there seemed no point in entering now; in fact, no point in doing anything until tomorrow was over. I made some tea. Angus came in and said, "I've tidied the midden and swept the whole yard. Did you see the letter from Geneva? It came by the late post!"

He gave it to me and I read it through, but nothing registered, because parties in Geneva and ambassadors and embassy officials' wives couldn't help us in any way with what lay ahead. That was all that mattered now.

"Perhaps we should have a drink," suggested Angus.

"No thank you," I answered, remembering how Geoff Craig had sat in Dad's chair, swilling whisky.

"Let's play Mastermind, then," he said.

I shook my head. "I'm not fit to play anything. I can't live again until tomorrow. My head aches and aches. I think I'm going to bed."

"But it's only six o'clock."

"I don't care," I said.

My bed was a haven from the world, a lair where I could hide from the dangers ahead. I didn't sleep, but lay trying not to think, and slowly the

65

minutes turned into hours. At eight o'clock Angus appeared with some hot chocolate and a bottle of aspirin.

"You aren't ill, are you? Shall I get the thermometer?" he asked.

"No, I'm just waiting for time to pass," I answered, and it was true.

Later I slept and wakened to a pale moon riding in a dark sky. Somewhere a cock was crowing, heralding another day.

I rose at five. The orchard was dappled with moonlight, but in the east the sun was rising. I made myself tea in the kitchen and boiled myself an egg, and felt courage coming back.

"We are going to succeed," I thought. "Tonight the horses will be home again and the nightmare will be finished."

7

At seven o'clock Angus appeared. He picked up
the post off the mat and held the letters to the
light.

"Nothing but bills," he said.

"You know Dad hates you doing that," I
answered. "Letters are meant to be private."

"Well, there's one for more than two figures."

"I expect it's the rates," I said.

I was now dressed in a hideous skirt I had found
in Mum's wardrobe, a polyester blouse I hated, a
ghastly blue cardigan, and some uncomfortable,
wedge-heeled sandals. I felt ugly and unpleasant,
a whiny female who nagged and wanted fags.

"You look terrific," Angus exclaimed. "I'm not
putting my moustache on until after breakfast."

"It would be funny if it wasn't so awful,"
I answered.

I had forced myself to eat the egg I had boiled,
and now I was waiting again for time to pass,
incapable of doing anything. Angus found my wig
and I put it on in front of the hall mirror. I looked
even worse with it on. Angus looked at me and
laughed.

"He'll never recognise you, Jean. I wouldn't
know you myself, you look so awful."

"Thank you," I said.

Angus looked quite handsome with his moustache, if you like moustaches. It was now eight o'clock, and I remembered my dark glasses.

"That's the final touch," said Angus, when I had put them on. "You look at least twenty-five and a real scrubber."

The shoes pinched my toes and I felt degraded, and knew that I wouldn't be able to look Dominic in the eye when he arrived.

At eight-fifteen I tripped outside in my hideous outfit to catch Phantom, but he took one look at me and fled. Round and round the orchard he galloped with his tail above his back, issuing ear-piercing snorts. Twilight followed, tiny and defiant.

I found a bucket of oats and called to him, but he wouldn't be caught. I took off my dark glasses and the wig and then he came cautiously, ready to flee at every step. I slipped a rope over his neck, talking to him all the time; then I put on our tattered headcollar and led him to the yard. Angus held him while I put on my wig and dark glasses again. Three minutes later Dominic arrived and burst out laughing when he saw us.

"Terrific," he cried. "I've never seen such a change. You look awful, Jean, absolutely ghastly. I don't think I'll call you my wife." He looked the same except for the hat, which made him appear older. He was full of energy, enjoying himself so much that I almost hated him.

Angus let down the ramp on the trailer. I spoke to Phantom and patted his neck. He followed me as far as the ramp and then stopped.

"He boxes all right, doesn't he?" asked Dominic anxiously.

"Usually," I answered.

Phantom stood looking around him, looking for Killarney, I thought, thinking that perhaps, like his friend, he wouldn't come back. It brought a lump to my throat. "It's all right," I said, feeling a traitor.

He followed me up in the end and Dominic gave a triumphant cheer. I tied him up and Angus threw up the ramp.

"We're on our way," cried Dominic, starting the engine. "And I've got a surprise for you, Jean," he added as I sat down beside him, and he sprayed me all over with scent. "You must smell right," he said, laughing. "Mum was given it for Christmas. It smells horrible—very cheap."

"It certainly suits the outfit," said Angus, opening a window.

"Oh, and fags. I've brought some for you," continued Dominic.

"You should be a stage manager," said Angus.

"Try smoking, Jean."

"I can't, I hate it."

"Try."

It was a terrible journey. Smoking made me cough and the boys were laughing and joking all the time as though we were going to a party rather than on a matter of life and death.

"By the way, the abattoirs *are* still on strike," said Dominic, after a time. "I heard it on the seven o'clock news, but they are going back tomorrow."

"So there's still only today," I said. "Just twenty-four hours."

"How do you know everything, Dominic?" asked Angus.

"I keep the radio on, even in the tractor. I hear the news every hour. The whole lot are out. Someone sacked a shop steward. There won't be any meat in the shops next week," replied Dominic. "And don't be so dramatic, Jean. You over-dramatise everything. We are going to save the horses, don't worry," he said.

"Touch wood."

There wasn't any wood in the Land Rover so I touched my head.

We stopped to buy some petrol, and Angus paid out of the housekeeping money, which was supposed to pay Mrs Parkin and keep us till our parents came back.

"Do cheer up, Jean," said Dominic, touching my arm. "This will soon be over."

But I couldn't cheer up. I felt a different person in my hideous clothes. I felt ugly and nasty inside and, at the same time, I was filled with nagging fears which gnawed at my stomach.

I wanted my parents to come home and take over, particularly Dad, who could use his influence in all sorts of places, and knew the right people, such as Chief Constables and magistrates.

I didn't trust Dominic and Angus to be a match for Geoff Craig and June. I didn't even trust myself.

We travelled through a town and there was sunlight everywhere—and a newspaper placard which read: '*Slaughter men go back tomorrow*.' I thought I couldn't take the money for Phantom, it would be physically impossible. But Dominic will take it. I wished that the sun would stop shining,

70

and I hated the happy people in the street, buying themselves spring outfits, lettuces and fruit. Then I started to feel sick.

Dominic looked at me anxiously. "We're nearly there. Open the window wider, Angus," he said.

"It isn't the Land Rover," I answered. "It's everything."

We left the town behind.

"He lives on a farm. Dad says it's a smart place with white rail fences and a brand-new house with a swimming-pool in front."

"Charming," said Angus.

"It can't be more than a mile from here," Dominic continued. "So let's stop and run through everything."

He parked in a lay-by.

I wanted to speak to Phantom, but Dominic was against it.

"You'll only cry," he said. "And we haven't much time. If we are late he will have gone out. I'm told he often plays golf in the mornings. Now, I am the owner of Phantom, OK? When I start talking, you switch on your recorder, Angus, right?"

"Right," agreed Angus.

"I shall offer him for sale. I shan't bother about a good home. I just want him got rid of quick because he's 'hot'—stolen."

"He should really have been stolen from us, then we would be sure to get him back," I answered.

"It's too late to change plans now," said Angus.

"You two must stand looking a bit goofy. Then, when Geoff Craig has incriminated himself, Angus slips off and calls the police. Look, there's a kiosk in front of us now, Angus, that will do."

"But supposing he wants to know where I've gone?" asked Angus.

"Don't worry, I'll handle that," replied Dominic.

"I don't seem to have anything to do," I complained.

"That doesn't matter. You are in reserve. Anything may happen," said Dominic, restarting the engine.

"I should have some reason to go," said Angus.

"Well, look here's a café and it's sure to have a telephone, so you can say, 'Mind if I go for some fags?', and slip away," suggested Dominic.

The café was a one-storey building with a petrol station in front. It was called the 'Wee Waif'. Lorries were parked on a lay-by opposite. Long net curtains hid the windows.

"Perfect," exclaimed Dominic. "Just right for us."

"My legs feel like string," said Angus.

We could see the house now, long and low, ranch-like, with a swimming-pool in front, a tennis court at the side, and four new loose boxes and an outdoor school. Beyond it all lay older buildings, including an enormous hangar big enough for Concorde, and a field full of horses of all sizes, and among them a grey with a familiar head.

"He's still there. Look," cried Angus in a shaky voice.

"Keep very calm," answered Dominic. "Don't panic."

"There's June," I cried. "Look, by the loose boxes."

"Remember who you are. My name is Jim Mallet and you're my wife, and he's Steve," said

Dominic, pointing at Angus, and now his voice was strained. Looking at him, I saw how tense he was, like a rubber band stretched as tight as it will go.

June was leading a bay thoroughbred out of a box as we stopped, and when Dominic jumped out and raised his hat, she called, "Dad's inside."

"You stay here," said Dominic, "but be ready with the recorder, Angus."

He looked at least twenty-four as he walked away. Angus held the tape-recorder. He had only to press a switch and everything Geoff Craig said would be recorded.

Dominic was banging on the front door now and my heart was thudding against my ribs.

Geoff Craig opened the door himself. "What is it?" he shouted. At the same time Angus stepped on to the drive and stood holding the recorder as though it was a radio.

"I've got a horse for sale. I hear you buy them," said Dominic, pointing at the trailer. "I don't want much for him."

They came towards us. I stayed in the cab of the Land Rover.

"Well, I've got plenty of horses as you can see, so the price must be right," said Geoff Craig.

"He's got plenty of flesh on him, but I don't want him to hang about, if you know what I mean," said Dominic.

"Oh, he's one of those is he?" replied Geoff Craig with a laugh. "You won't get much then."

"I lifted him straight out of a field. I had to cut the padlock. It's getting harder all the time," continued Dominic.

"What is he then—a palomino?" asked Geoff Craig, peering into the trailer.

"Yes, would you like me to get him out for you? I haven't seen much of him myself, because it was dark when I fetched him," said Dominic.

"No, don't bother. I can see enough from here. I don't really want him anyway. You can see how many I've got already and the abattoir can't handle more than twenty a day."

"I'd better be going then," said Dominic, while Angus looked uncertain what to do.

"I'll tell you what. I'll give you two hundred and fifty, which, seeing that he's stolen, is a pretty good price."

"Done," said Dominic. "Where shall I put him?"

"Come in first and get the money. Is that your girl-friend in the Land Rover?"

"Wife."

"I'll just slip down to the café for some fags, all right, Jim?" asked Angus.

"OK, Steve," said Dominic.

"Well, bring her along too and we might be able to hustle up some coffee," suggested Geoff Craig.

My legs were shaking as I stepped on to the drive. Dominic took my arm. "She's just getting over the flu and she's still a bit weak on her legs," he said.

Mrs Craig greeted us when we reached the house. She said, "Pleased to meet you," and held out a small hand.

The sitting-room was full of silver cups. There wasn't a book to be seen, only *Horse and Hound* on a low coffee-table.

"How did you hear of me then?" asked Geoff Craig.

"Through a farmer friend, can't remember his name. He said he had sold you a horse or two," replied Dominic.

I groped for my cigarettes because I didn't know what to do with my hands.

"Do you want a light?" asked Geoff Craig.

My hands were shaking so much that he said, "You wife is cold, we had better put some heat on. She's very poorly, isn't she?"

"She suffers from nerves," said Dominic with the trace of a smile.

We drank coffee out of expensive cups while Geoff Craig gave Dominic a handful of notes, saying, "Count them, there should be two hundred and fifty there."

I looked at the notes and I thought—just a few bits of paper for a horse, how can people do it?

Dominic was standing up now. "All fair and square. Thank you very much, Mr Craig."

"Not at all, if you have any more the same, I'll buy them any time," he said.

"That's a deal, sir," replied Dominic, holding out his hand.

They shook hands and Geoff Craig said, "Now you look after that wife of yours, Jim, she doesn't look at all well to me."

Dominic answered, "Nerves are the very devil. Where do you want me to put the horse, sir?"

We stood reflected in the swimming-pool while he said, "Over there in the hangar. I want him out of sight."

"Yes, sir," said Dominic.

"What now?" I asked as we reached the trailer.

"The police haven't arrived. What about Phantom?"

"Hop in," said Dominic. "They're watching us."

We drove down the drive and stopped by the hangar. It was surrounded by old pieces of motor cars and broken tractors. The doors were locked.

"The key is on the ground under a stone," shouted Geoff Craig.

"Do you think they are alive inside?" I asked.

"Of course," replied Dominic, searching for the key.

"I'm scared," I said.

"You're always scared. Where's your courage?"

"It's not your horse going in there," I answered. I stared down the drive. There was no sign of anyone.

"I can't see Angus," I said.

"It's five minutes' walk to the café," said Dominic.

He had found the key. He waved it in the direction of the house and we heard the front door slam.

"Now for the doors," he said.

"And goodbye Phantom," I answered.

"Don't be melodramatic," said Dominic. "Here comes June."

8

She called, "What are you doing there? This is private property."

Dominic straightened his back and looked at her.

"It's all right, miss," he answered. "We've just seen your Dad. It's all above board."

She was beautifully turned out and so was her horse. I felt her sizing me up, despising what she saw. I looked down the drive and saw Angus coming back. He waved and called, "They're coming presently."

June asked, "Who is they?" I had to admit she was quick on the uptake.

"He's my mate. He's invited some pals to meet us in the café up the road. It's not every day I've got two hundred and fifty quid in my pocket."

"I know his voice," she said, riding towards Angus.

"Hey, miss, he's married," shouted Dominic laughing, but his laughter sounded false. "Come on, get Phantom out quick," he said.

We backed Phantom out, but he wouldn't approach the hangar. Angus came running towards us, crying "Want a hand, mate?"

"I know you," cried June. "So you must know me."

"I've never set eyes on you before," said Angus.

"Miss," hissed Dominic.

"Miss," added Angus.

I gave Angus Phantom's headcollar-rope and slipped into the hangar. It was full of horses and ponies of all shapes and sizes. Most of them looked bewildered and two were no more than foals. Three whinnied and came up to me, so obviously begging to be released that I found it difficult not to cry.

There was plenty of hay at the far end and a trough of water, so it was obvious that they weren't meant to lose weight while under sentence of death.

I felt like pulling off my wig and screaming at June, "I know you, your murderess." But now Angus and Dominic were pushing Phantom into the hangar inch by inch, and my worst nightmare was coming true.

"Coax him, Jean," hissed Dominic.

And I whispered, "I can't. I can't betray him like that."

I was crying. June had dismounted and was staring at us with hostility and perplexity fairly mixed on her face.

Angus slammed the door behind Phantom, banging his hocks. "That's that," he said.

Inside the hangar, we all looked at each other in alarm.

"For heaven's sake, let's get out of here, she knows we are pretenders," said Dominic.

"Supposing they try and beat us up—where's the tape-recorder?" said Dominic.

"Buried in the groom's compartment. I'm not a fool," said Angus.

"What did the police say?" asked Dominic.

"That they would investigate. They said that there was nothing wrong with the horse meat trade. I think they respect Geoff Craig," explained Angus with awful gloom in his voice.

"We can't stay here," said Dominic.

"What are we going to do, then?" I asked. "These ponies are probably all stolen. Tomorrow most of them will be killed and there will be no evidence left, just the meat on its way to the continent. Couldn't you make them understand?"

"I tried. If I could have met them face to face it might have been different, but there was a man tapping on the side of the kiosk all the time and that didn't help."

"Oh God, we've failed," cried Dominic. "Let's get out of here and think."

I left Phantom and we stepped outside, slamming the doors after us. I could see Killarney grazing less than fifty yards away, and neither of them were ours any more.

June was waiting for us outside the hangar. She said: "Your wig is coming off, Jean. Why are you dressed up? What do you want?"

"Nothing," replied Dominic.

"Look down there at your Land Rover. The two men there are waiting to beat you up. They are ex-convicts. There won't be much left of you when they've finished," she said.

"Charming," replied Angus, and I saw that his moustache had slipped. "But how can you live like this, watching horses and ponies go for slaughter?"

"What do you mean?" she asked.

"Well, you love horses, don't you? Or is it all a pretence?" asked Angus. "And isn't living so close to those condemned rather like living next to a concentration camp and the gas chamber?"

"How do you feel when you see them leave?" asked Dominic. "Doesn't it hurt you? Or are you so hard you don't care?"

"Of course I care," she said. I knew by her voice that she was cracking. "I hate the trade, but I can't change Dad. He's made all his money out of it. I can ride because of the business. We live in comfort. He's risen up in the world—he's a member of the golf club. What do you expect me to do, go to the police?"

"Can't you talk to him?" I asked.

"No one can talk to him," she replied simply.

"I'm sorry," said Dominic.

"What for?"

"For you."

"Well, I'm sorry for you," she answered, and I could see a tear smudging her mascara, "because you're going to be in a sorry state soon, when those two down there have finished with you."

"The police will deal with them," said Angus.

"Dad has the police eating out of his hand," she answered with a bitter laugh. "You won't get any help from them. I'm sorry I can't help you. If you had come to me first, I might have saved Killarney, but it's too late now, both of them will go for meat in the morning. He won't keep them a minute longer than necessary, you can be sure of that."

"Thanks for telling us," said Dominic.

"You're welcome."

Angus and Dominic looked at one another.

"Sharpen your fists," said Dominic. "I hope you know judo."

Angus shook his head and bent down to pick up a discarded fencing post. "I'll use this," he said.

"Get in the Land Rover and keep out of the fight, Jean," said Dominic. "This is between us and *them*."

"You are no match for *them*," I answered.

June rode away. She stopped to talk to the two men as she passed and we heard them laugh, as though they were looking forward to the fight ahead.

"Here we go," said Dominic.

"I'm going to get Phantom," I said. I ran back to the hangar but the door was locked. I suppose it was a self-locking one. I looked for the key under the appropriate stone but it wasn't there. We must have dropped it inside. Then I was running after the boys, praying, "God, don't let them be hurt, please, God."

They looked small and light compared with the two ex-convicts, like two whippets taking on a pair of bloodhounds. As they drew near I heard Geoff Craig call, "Don't break any bones, just beat them up good and proper." He was standing on his doorstep, holding an Alsatian, and his wife stood just behind, looking over his shoulder.

I thought, there's no help coming. We are on our own. Dominic and Angus had nearly reached the Land Rover. I thought—go for their legs, Jean, try a rugger tackle—and I remembered Dad teaching me to fight years ago.

June was putting her horse away, rubbing him down as though she loved him, while the ponies in the hangar awaited death—children's beloved ponies, foals newly weaned from their mothers, old hunters who had always done their best across country, even show ponies worth far more than Geoff Craig had paid. Only we could save them now.

I prayed for strength and courage and now the boys had reached the men. Angus went straight down and his attacker raised his foot and kicked him. I screamed, "No! Stop it. No." I ran towards them, my own fear forgotton, thinking only of Angus lying doubled up in pain.

I threw myself at the man, suddenly conscious of how light I was and I yelled, "You'll go to prison for this. Stop kicking my brother."

He turned and at the same moment Dominic sprang at him. I saw that the other man was lying on the ground and I knew that there was still hope left.

"Get into the Land Rover and start the engine, Jean," yelled Dominic.

Angus scrambled to his feet and leapt inside too. He seized the wheel and at the same moment I heard Geoff Craig yelling: "What are you doing? I said to beat them up."

Then Dominic was in the Land Rover with us and we were flying down the drive towards the house at sixty miles an hour. We turned the trailer in the yard and saw that the men were waiting for us, blocking the drive. Dominic moved into the driver's seat and seized the steering-wheel.

"Don't kill them," shouted Angus nervously, as we raced towards them. "I don't want a life sentence."

Dominic opened his window long enough to shout, "Move or you'll be dead." Then miraculously the way was clear and I saw that Angus's face was red with blood and his moustache had gone.

Dominic looked in the mirror. "They are following us. We're not in the clear yet," he said.

"Head for the nearest town. We need people," said Angus in a shaky voice, as we swung into the road.

I looked back and saw a Mercedes following us. It was trying to overtake us but there were too many cars coming in the other direction. Dominic had the accelerator as far down as it would go. His face was grim and he was using swear words I had never heard before. Then we heard a tyre burst.

"It's all right, it's only on the trailer. It doesn't matter," he said.

I thought, if only our horses were inside, and my heart was aching for Phantom.

We heard another tyre burst and Angus said unnecessarily, "They are shooting." I thought, they can't be, not in broad daylight. But no-one seemed to bother. Perhaps they just didn't want to get involved, or maybe, they thought we were having a succession of blow-outs.

"Where are the police?" asked Angus.

"Handing out parking-tickets," replied Dominic.

We stopped behind a bus. Now there were people everywhere, sane, ordinary people carrying plastic bags, pushing prams, walking arm in arm.

"We had better park. We are safer in a crowd," suggested Dominic.

"On a double yellow line," I added, "because then the police may appear."

But the police didn't appear. The Mercedes stopped behind us and the two ex-convicts got out.

"Supposing they shoot at us," I asked.

"They won't, not here in the street," answered Angus.

Dominic opened his window. "Why don't you just buzz off?" he asked.

"You won't get off so easily. We know where you live. So just keep your mouths shut, OK?" one said.

I looked at them properly for the first time. One had dark hair and a sharp nose, and he hadn't shaved for some time. The other was completely bald.

I was too petrified to speak, but Angus answered, "Thanks for telling us," in a cheeky voice.

"You wouldn't want a bomb through the letter-box of your little cottage, now, would you? So just keep your sweet little mouths shut, do you hear?"

"We hear," Dominic replied.

They banged on the Land Rover roof with their fists before leaving. Dominic said, "Well, that's that, then." He turned the ignition.

"I am not scared for myself," he said a moment later, "but I am for you, because they know where you live. I think you had better send for your parents."

"We can't. They are busy. Besides, it's babyish to send for Mum and Dad the minute things get bad," I answered.

"You were marvellous," said Angus. "You saved our lives. I had no idea you knew judo."

"Yes. I used to go to evening classes," replied Dominic. "I advise you to do the same, seeing that you seem bent on getting into trouble . . ."

Suddenly it seemed years since morning.

"They could burn you in your beds," continued Dominic. "I think we should go the the police again—to our police. They might keep an eye on your place. You need protection."

"You sound so serious, I can't believe it's as bad as that," said Angus.

"I think it is," replied Dominic.

I thought of sending for our parents. I imagined them packing their bags, their faces creased with worry. We should have gone with them, I thought.

"June is human after all," said Angus.

"Just," answered Dominic. "You had better come to my place for lunch. It's twelve o'clock, and I don't suppose you've got a thing prepared."

"Don't worry, Mrs Parkin will have been," said Angus. "We are well organised, the freezer is stacked to the top with food."

"You can stay with us for tonight. You must," said Dominic. "Mum and Dad will insist."

"It's cowardly," answered Angus.

"No, it isn't, it's common sense."

But the torments of the day weren't over yet. When we reached our cottage the orchard was empty. We rushed to the paddock, but there was no Twilight.

"As if things aren't bad enough," I cried.

"I expect he's with his mum by now. Don't worry," said Dominic. "I'll go and look, and ring you back in five minutes."

"You've done enough," replied Angus, as he drove away.

I rushed upstairs and tore off my hideous clothes and put on jeans, a sweater and washed my face. The cottage felt empty. Mrs Parkin had left a note

85

which read: '*Out again! Your dinner is in the oven. I took my wages from the usual place. I hope this is all right. It was all the money there.*' Mrs P.

Angus served lunch. I felt as though I had come to the end of everything, that there was no hope. Killarney and Phantom would be slaughtered in the morning, and that would be the end. If the police won't help, we're finished, I thought. And I shall never have another horse; I won't want one either, not after Phantom. And it is all our fault because if Angus hadn't decided to sell Killarney it wouldn't have happened, and if I hadn't willed Killarney to go lame, he could have had a lovely home. So we are both to blame.

Then the telephone rang. It was Dominic. "Don't worry," he said. "Twilight *is* here and I've put him with his mum again, so he'll be all right. And Dad's going to the police when we've eaten. They'll listen to him, and you're expected here tonight, OK?"

"OK," I answered.

Angus had washed the blood off his face, but it was swollen on one side and one of his teeth was broken.

He said, 'OK' too. I put down the receiver.

Another day had nearly gone and we still hadn't rescued Killarney, and tomorrow the abattoirs would be open again.

"We will have to go there tomorrow," I said.

"Where?"

"To the abattoir, of course," I answered.

After that I slept with my head on the kitchen table and dreamed that Phantom had come home. He was standing in the yard, neighing, with the setting sun behind him, and I was filled with a

86

great happiness. "I knew he would return," I said, and felt him nudge my arm, but it was only Angus shaking me, saying, "Wake up. It's time to go to the farm." And I knew that the nightmare was still there, not over yet—perhaps with us for ever.

9

The farm felt very safe. Mrs Barnes had made up a bed for me in one of the attic rooms and I could see Sparrow Cottage from the window, small and neat in the valley. Angus had a camp-bed in Dominic's room.

Mr Barnes had been to the police. "They are looking into the matter," he said. "I told them everything. It's not in their area, but they are contacting the appropriate police force."

"But they can't stop our horses going to be killed, because we sold them," I answered.

"They can stop Phantom, because I sold him and he was stolen. It's all on the tape, isn't it? Listen, I'll play it to you," said Dominic. "It's in Dad's safe. You left it in the trailer."

He fetched the recorder and we sat and listened to it in the homely farm kitchen, and all the horror came back to me.

"You've turned white," said Dominic, switching it off.

I couldn't stop shivering. Mrs Barnes led me to the attic bedroom. "You slip into bed between the sheets," she said. "There's a hot water-bottle there, so you won't be cold, and one of us will bring you supper on a tray."

She drew the curtains, shutting out Sparrow Cottage and the spring evening. "Now don't worry, my duck, everything will be all right," she said. I wished that I could believe her, but I couldn't.

I was certain now that the ex-convicts would kill Phantom, rather than let us buy him back, because he was our best piece of evidence—the only real link between the tape and Geoff Craig.

Suddenly everything seemed hopeless. Then Dominic came in with a tray, sat on my bed and said, "Trust us. Everything is going to be all right, Jean. I promise."

There was steak and kidney pie on the tray, with peas and mashed potatoes, and cake, bread and butter and chocolate mousse. I didn't feel like any of it. I saw that Dominic had a swollen lip and there were shadows under his eyes which hadn't been there before. He took my hand and said, "Eat it up, Jean, please. By tomorrow night everything will be all right." Then he left me, running downstairs to the kitchen below.

I tried to eat, but the food turned to sawdust in my mouth. Presently Angus appeared and said, "Why don't you eat it? Can't you see you're upsetting Mrs Barnes? It's rude to leave things. Haven't you any manners?" He looked hideous with half a tooth missing, and I thought—our parents will never leave us alone after this.

"Eat it up and then come and watch telly. There's a super film on. One of us will come back in five minutes to collect the tray. Don't be wet, Jean," pleaded Angus.

I ate most of it and then sat watching television without seeing anything, imagining instead the inside of the abattoir, full of carcasses dripping blood, horse's heads, and among them Phantom's, pale gold, severed, but still beautiful.

Mr Barnes sat with his braces lying in his lap, and Mrs Barnes continually asked questions like, "Why did he do that?" and, "Which side is he on Dominic, I can't remember." Outside, rain fell furiously, lashing the window-panes.

At intervals tears blinded my vision and Dominic looked at me anxiously and asked, "All right, Jean?" I muttered, "Yes, of course," in a voice muffling uncontrollable sobs, and so, slowly, the evening passed, one of the worst I can remember.

At ten o'clock Mrs Barnes brought us hot drinks on a tray—cocoa, hot milk and Ovaltine.

Angus was very polite. "We can't thank you enough," he said, while Mr Barnes looked at the tray and then mixed himself a whisky and soda. I thought, this time tomorrow it will all be over—either we will have saved our horses or they will be dead. I imagined life without Phantom and it felt as empty as a deserted building, and just as pointless.

Mrs Barnes patted me on the shoulder. "Have a good sleep, Jean," she said, "and everything will seem better in the morning."

I wanted to say 'you hope', but it didn't seem a polite answer to a middle-aged person, so I said, "Thank you," instead.

When I reached my attic bedroom the rain had stopped and the night was clear and full of stars.

"Don't worry, Jean," said Angus. "Everything is going to be all right."

"I seem to have heard you say that before," I answered. "I just wish our parents were here. They would know what to do, who to ring up. The Barnes are sweet, but they don't know much, do they?"

"The police have taken over now," replied Angus.

"Why are we going to the abattoir then?" I asked.

"To be certain to save Killarney. Phantom is safe."

But I didn't believe him any more, nor Dominic, nor anyone.

"You promised Phantom would be all right and he isn't," I replied. "We were going to bring him back yesterday—remember? And is he here? No. He's with all the other stolen horses ready to go in the morning."

Angus looked at me. "OK, it's my fault, I know, and if they both die I shall carry their deaths on my conscience for ever." He shut the door after him and I heard his feet despondently on the stairs below. I thought—it's no good blaming anyone, it was probably fate. But it didn't seem that way.

My bed was old and creaky, and the ceiling sloped above my head. I imagined the people who had slept in the room before me—farm labourers with gnarled hands, girls who helped in the kitchen, milkmaids perhaps, the farmer's children. I imagined them coming to bed by candlelight.

The wallpaper had roses on it and I tried counting them, but nothing stopped me imagining the abattoir, until sometime in the middle of the night when I must have slept, for the next thing I heard was a chorus of cocks crowing and the sound of cloven hooves passing below my window. I looked out and saw Dominic driving the cows towards the milking parlour with two dogs at his heels. Dawn was breaking in the east and the whole yard was full of the songs of birds.

Today we go to the abattoir again, I thought, and they won't be on strike this time. The thought filled me with horror. Soon afterwards there was a timid tap on my bedroom door and Mrs Barnes came in with tea on a tray. The teapot was covered with a cosy and there was a flowered sugar basin, milk jug, and cup and saucer to match.

"There's no hurry, my duck," she said. "Dominic is out milking, but he'll be in for breakfast at seven. So just you come down when you're ready."

She was wearing her pinny, bedroom slippers, thick stockings, and a sweater and skirt. She looked tired to death.

I said, "Thank you very much, but you shouldn't have done it, Mrs Barnes. I don't want to be a nuisance."

"You couldn't be a nuisance if you tried, Jean," she replied, leaving the room.

I imagined myself being a prosperous middle-aged lady as I sat in bed, drinking tea, but all the time at the back of my mind horror lurked, waiting to rush in. I drew back the curtains and the sky was clear with only a hint of dawn left. There was a clanging noise coming from the milking parlour and the hum of machinery driven by electricity. Half a mile away, Sparrow Cottage looked small and silent beneath the early sun, and the ploughed land was tinged green with growing wheat.

I dressed, and found breakfast ready on the large table in the kitchen.

"Tea or coffee, Jean? And help yourself to cereal," said Mrs Barnes.

"Coffee, please, you're spoiling me," I answered, as Angus came bounding into the kitchen saying, "What a lovely day, Mrs Barnes."

Then Dominic appeared and washed at the old-fashioned stone sink. "Twilight's as happy as a sandboy," he said.

I ate a large breakfast without tasting any of it, while Angus made bright conversation and Dominic looked at my face from time to time. I avoided his eye, hating both him and Angus because they had caused me to sell Phantom. Mr Barnes came in next, full of farm news, of kittens born in the barn, and a cow with mastitis, which drove him to the telephone.

"It's always something, isn't it?" said Mrs Barnes in a weary voice. "Don't you ever marry a farmer, Jean."

Dominic ate five rashers of bacon and two eggs. "We leave at eight," he said, buttering toast so thickly that the toast looked likely to collapse under the weight. "The abattoir isn't opening until nine-thirty because they've got to get things going again after the strike. Dad telephoned them. They say they don't buy stolen horses."

You had better get that tooth fixed, Angus," said Mr Barnes, coming back. "The vet will be here directly, Mother," he added to his wife.

We carried our plates to the sink. I had the pain in my stomach which comes before you go into the ring at a horse show and I was doing everything automatically, like a zombie.

Dominic smoothed his hair in front of the mirror by the sink and put on a jacket.

"No need for disguise today," he said, smiling without joy. "Are you ready?"

"I feel as though I'm going to my execution," remarked Angus, as we stepped outside.

"It's almost the same, only it's Phantom's," I answered.

"Now don't you get in any trouble," called Mrs Barnes. "Do you hear, Dominic? You're the eldest, so I'll hold you responsible if things go wrong . . ."

The trailer was still hitched to the Land Rover, the flat tyres changed for new ones. I sat in the middle between the boys, staring at the dashboard. Dominic started the engine. The cows were going back to pasture, slowly, like old women.

"I'm afraid," I said. "Just terribly, terribly afraid."

"We are going to win," said Angus, without conviction.

"We can't lose," said Dominic, with even less.

We passed Sparrow Cottage.

"We should have left a message for Mrs P.," remembered Angus.

"Do you want to stop?"

"No, there isn't time. We'll ring up when it's over," Angus answered.

"Will she be anxious?"

"I don't know."

Energetic men were walking dogs before driving to work. A woman was riding a bay horse. It was like any other morning; it wasn't marked in any way, or scarred by what might happen. It was the sort of morning you dream about when you're far away—an April morning in England with the sap rising and flowers as common as grass.

"Let's sing," suggested Angus after a time, and

94

then started droning, "Ten Green Bottles Hanging on the Wall".

"After this is over we must meet more often," said Dominic. "Do you agree?"

I nodded.

"It's silly to live so near one another and hardly see each other from one month to the next," he continued. "And you both ride better than me. I can only sit on over sticks. I don't know anything about real riding."

"Nonsense," replied Angus.

I knew we were just filling in time, trying to detach our minds from what lay ahead. We were all frightened of failure, so frightened that we couldn't mention it, so we kept up a bright, pointless conversation to keep our minds occupied.

Then, at last, Dominic turned to me and said, "Only five more miles now, Jean." His face was pale and tense, but understanding, and I thought, he's in this too, right to the hilt.

10

We reached the abattoir. Beyond it, the river banks were dotted with daffodils. Dominic stopped the Land Rover. There were three cattle trucks parked outside and a horse neighing in the distance. The river was hardly moving.

"It's very quiet," said Angus.

The doors were metal, the kind which slide back.

"Shall I knock?" asked Dominic. "You needn't get near, Jean. Keep away. You'll only get upset."

"He might be inside," I replied. "I must look."

"You'll only faint if he is. Women always do," said Angus.

"How do you know?"

"I just do."

"We wouldn't be here if it wasn't for you," I answered bitterly.

"This is no time for bickering," said Dominic, stepping on to the tarmac.

We followed him, my heart beating like a revved-up engine, Angus as tense as taut wire, his face full of anguish.

Dominic knocked, and we waited for what seemed like five minutes but was probably five seconds, and they were the longest seconds of my life.

Then a man in a white coat slid back the doors. And inside there were carcasses hanging, men cutting them into joints, innards neatly hanging from hooks on a trolley. I felt my legs turn to jelly, for Phantom could be hanging there, stripped of his golden coat, waiting to be sent to feed the lions in a wildlife park, his hooves turned to glue, his skin turned into a coat. It was more than I could bear. My eyes refused to focus any more. Then I could feel Dominic holding me up.

"I'm all right, I'm only fainting," I said, while my mind searched for some piece of Phantom, at the same time praying, "Please, God, let him be alive."

The man must have said something, to which Angus answered. "She's anaemic, always has been," in furious tones.

The abattoir man replied, "She should see a doctor then."

His voice came to me from a long way off. Everything was tiny and far away like when you look down the wrong end of binoculars. Then it wasn't there at all.

When I came to, we were moving again. I sat up. "I smell of the abattoir," I cried.

"You shouldn't faint. We had to carry you," Angus answered.

The speedometer read sixty-five miles an hour.

"You mean *he* did—the man at the abattoir?"

They nodded. "He insisted," said Dominic. I thought of him carrying carcasses.

"He can't help the work he does," replied Angus, "Someone has to do it."

I asked, "Was he there? Did you check? Ask if they had had a palomino in recently?"

"Yes. And they had," replied Angus, looking out of the window at green trees and fields where Phantom might have gone on living.

"There are thousands of palominos in the world," said Dominic. "It needn't have been Phantom."

"Where are we going?" I asked next, wiping my eyes.

"To Geoff Craig's."

"Why?"

"Because I want to kill him," Angus replied.

I tried to understand. "Was Killarney there, then?" I asked at last.

"No, he wasn't. I want to be sick," Angus said suddenly.

Dominic stopped the Land Rover. Sweat was running down his face. I thought—it's a kind face, but strong too, perhaps the kindest one I've ever seen.

Angus finished being sick and climbed back into the Land Rover. He looked very white.

"How far is it?" I asked.

"Another twenty miles. We are going to save both horses. We've had enough. We're going to take them home," cried Dominic.

"We don't care if we go to prison. We only want to save them," added Angus.

"I shall go too. I want to," I answered, imagining myself in prison clothes, a wardress with jangling keys, a cell with nothing in it but a bed.

"You're being melodramatic," replied Dominic, stopping the Land Rover outside the Wee Waif Café.

"I don't understand," I said. "What if neither of them are there?"

"We have no proof either way," answered Dominic.

"We're going the rest of the way on foot," explained Angus, looking at me with red-rimmed eyes.

"And then into the hangar," added Dominic.

"If we can't find the key we're going to climb in," said Angus.

"And we want you to stay behind. You can send for help if we need it," Dominic told me.

"Phantom will only move for Jean. He's a one-man horse," said Angus, climbing out of the Land Rover.

"He won't be there," I said.

"Angus, you stay behind then," suggested Dominic, as though I hadn't spoken. "We need *someone* to stay behind."

"Not me though, because I must be the one to suffer, because it was all my fault in the first place," answered Angus.

"Well, I must go because I'm the only one who knows judo," said Dominic with a sigh.

So finally we crossed the road together, before ducking under a barbed wire fence, and we felt horribly exposed as we crossed the field between us and the hangar.

"If they look out they can see us," said Angus.

"We can't run doubled up or we will look suspicious," replied Dominic.

"He won't be there," I said again.

"Shut up!" cried Angus. "Just shut up."

I thought—supposing they shoot? Supposing they're waiting for us when we reach the hangar? We were looking at the huge, grey building where the horses waited, doomed to die. And I think we were all frightened inside ourselves; though we tried to appear unafraid. Inside we were just three frightened people.

"I'll go for the key," said Dominic, and was gone before we could stop him, doubled up, sliding under a fence into the yard beyond.

I looked at Angus and saw nothing but fear on his face. I looked at the hangar. It was built of brick and breeze-blocks.

Angus said, "They must have seen us. We were visible at least three times when we crossed the field. Anyone looking out of the house . . ."

"Don't let's talk," I pleaded. There was an empty feeling in the pit of my stomach and my right hand wouldn't stop shaking.

"No luck," said Dominic, returning.

"Did anyone see you?" asked Angus.

"I don't know."

"What are we going to do now?" I asked.

"Climb in," replied Dominic. "It's our only hope."

We stood and stared at the hangar.

"What about getting out?" I asked.

"*If* we get in?" added Angus.

"We will wait till someone comes, then I'll leap up behind you and we'll be off," replied Dominic.

"What about headcollars?" asked Angus.

"There's a pile by the door. I'll get two," replied Dominic.

"Why you?" I asked.

"Because I know judo."

"We're letting him take all the risks," I said.

A few seconds later Angus was climbing up the hangar. There was a space between the breeze-blocks and the roof, and there were footholds between the breeze-blocks, but it wasn't easy. When he reached the top he tied the headcollar-ropes to a support so that there was a loop to help us up.

"You next," said Dominic. "Climb on to my shoulders, then reach for the rope."

I stood on Dominic's shoulders, grabbed the loop and for an awful second I swung until my feet found the breeze-blocks.

"I'll pull you up," said Angus.

I scraped my knees on the rough surface, then somehow I was astride the wall. Dominic was climbing easily, like someone who knows the way by instinct, while my knees felt sticky with blood. I thought of my parents. I imagined them coming back to find us dead, our heads smashed to pieces by Geoff Craig's thugs. I wondered whether they would ever know the real story.

"Over the top," said Dominic, arriving beside us, "then down into the hangar. Slide and then jump. There's only peat and horse dung below."

My head was bent to avoid the roof. I twisted myself round and hung for a moment with the smell of horse stronger than I had ever smelt it before in my nostrils. Then I let go and hit the wet peat with my shoulder, before leaping to my feet. Almost at once I heard a whinny. Another second, and I was standing with my arms round Phantom's neck, crying bucketfuls into his mane and whispering, "Thank God you're alive ... Thank God ..." And Angus was putting a headcollar on Killarney's wise grey head, and I knew he was crying too.

While Dominic tried the doors, I looked at the other horses and wished I could save them all.

There was a chestnut soaked in sweat who walked up and down like a tiger in a cage, and a dun pony who nudged my back in a familiar way and then started to search my pockets for a titbit. There was a roan which had been hurt and lay with a wound bleeding on to the dirty bedding, and a foal which could have been born in the last half-hour, tottering to his feet while his mother licked him with her tongue. There was a large black horse with grey hairs round his eyes and a little bay mare with an Arab head . . . They all pulled at my heart-strings. There were others, too, standing together, resting legs; plain bays and browns, a funny spotted roan with a wall-eye and three little Shetlands . . .

I was still looking at them when Dominic said, "It's no good, I can't open the doors. No way."

"We'll mount, then . . ." said Angus.

I vaulted on to Phantom and wondered how long we would have to wait, my heart thudding against my ribs again.

Then we heard the sound of glass breaking outside. It continued for some time, and after that Geoff Craig laughed and cracked a joke; and I thought I heard June's voice say, "Well done, Dad . . ."

I looked at the others. "What is it?" I whispered.

"I don't know."

"I'm scared," whispered Angus.

"Be ready . . ." said Dominic.

I got ready like one does before a bending race, but there were no poles and no cheering crowds, just the dirty hangar and the sad, doomed horses and the two boys who suddenly looked what they were—two three-quarter-grown adolescents incapable of fighting twelve-stone men. My heart was in my boots. Then Angus said, "Listen," and in the distance we heard the wailing of a police car.

Dominic said, "Well done, Dad. He's sent help at last."

I kissed Phantom and said, "Soon you'll be free," and I didn't touch wood.

We heard a car racing up the drive, the screech of brakes, and then Geoff Craig's voice shouting, "They're over in the hangar . . ." And suddenly we knew everything had gone terribly wrong.

"I locked them in," he shouted. "They've smashed all the windows, look, over there. It's not the first time, I'm telling you. I'm sick of vandalism . . ."

Then we heard the voice of a police officer saying, "It's happening all over the country, sir. You're not the only one to suffer."

I could feel the blood draining from my face, and I couldn't look at Angus for fear of what I might read on his.

"It's a frame-up. But don't worry, we'll win. Don't give up, whatever happens," said Dominic. The strain in his voice terrified me even more.

We heard the key in the padlock and the chain being pulled through the catch.

"There's nothing to be frightened of," said Dominic, "because we're innocent . . ."

"Famous last words," said Angus.

"I'm thinking of Phantom," I said. "Supposing I never see him again?"

"If it wasn't for the horses I wouldn't care," said Angus.

The door opened and the police rushed in, dragging us off our horses, refusing to let us speak, treating us like criminals, and, as we were hauled out of that ghastly hangar, we could see June watching with her father, and that was almost the worst thing of all.

Angus looked at her and spat out one word, "Murderess . . ."

As I was pushed into the police car I remembered her coming to Sparrow Cottage, and how Angus had waited on her, and I could feel bitterness in my throat burning like acid.

There were two police cars. I was put in one with an officer sitting beside me, while the boys went together in another. All I could think of as we drove away was June's face, and I imagined it filled with triumph.

I looked at the police officer beside me, and I said, "There's been a mistake."

He said, "They all say that, love. Keep your lies to yourself until we reach the station."

No one had ever treated me in the same way before.

"It isn't true," I said after a time. "We didn't break anything. We were trying to rescue our horses . . ."

"Well, that's a new line anyway, love," he said after a short silence, and looked at me for the first time.

"It's the truth. And my father is quite important," I added. "I'm not a hooligan . . ."

"Important, is he?" asked the officer, and laughed.

"And we didn't break the glass," I added, my courage increasing.

"Who did then?"

"Mr Craig," I answered.

He laughed again. I thought of Phantom being loaded, tied up, driven to the abattoir; and I thought—he won't go in, he'll fight every inch of the way. It was like a small glimmer of hope.

11

A small crowd stopped to watch us being bundled into the police station.

Dominic protested loudly. "I'm a farmer's son. I live forty miles from here. Why don't you check up? My Land Rover is parked by the Wee Waif Café. The number is POW 905," he said.

Inside the police station we were told to wait. There were benches, a policeman by the door, no escape. I thought of Phantom. Where was he now?

"How long will we be here?" I asked, but no one answered. The clock above the door told us it was one o'clock, later than I thought.

"Do you think the abattoir shuts for lunch?" I asked.

Dominic nodded. His face looked hard and strong—and dirty. Angus was biting his nails.

"What a mess," said Dominic after a time.

"You're so right," answered Angus. "I never thought the police could be so stupid. Do we look like vandals?"

"I don't know. I've never seen one," I said. "I'm thinking about Phantom, about him dying, because they won't keep him now."

"And Killarney, and about it all being my fault," replied Angus.

"It's no good crying over spilt milk," said Dominic. "Why don't they hurry up? One call to my father and the whole thing could be cleared up in minutes."

"Exactly," cried Angus.

We all stood up without thinking. Dominic approached the constable by the door.

"What's the hold-up, officer?" he said.

"We're waiting for the superintendent."

"Meanwhile our horses die," I said.

"I don't know anything about that."

We sat down again.

"They will have to kill him there, because he won't load. He only loads for me," I said.

"They won't do that. They like meat fresh for the abattoir," replied Dominic with a twisted smile.

"But they'll have Killarney. He loads for anyone," said Angus.

I imagined them struggling with Phantom. I imagined him on the ground, leaping to his feet, twisting, kicking, rearing. I imagined ropes round his quarters, blindfolds over his eyes, whips cracking, stones flying; and as I imagined, tears ran down my cheeks like rain.

Dominic looked at me and said, "Don't give up, Jean. While there's life there's hope."

"They won't think we'll have the courage to go back," said Angus. "They'll be complacent now."

"It's a long walk back to the Land Rover," I answered.

"I shall ring my father. He will give the police hell. We'll be driven back, don't worry," answered Dominic. "They'll be sorry they ever picked us up by the time he's finished with them."

I imagined Mr Barnes answering the telephone, Mrs Barnes behind him, listening; the cows outside drifting towards the farm because it would soon be milking time. Mrs Parkin would have been to Sparrow Cottage, tidied up, and left another of her messages. And, far away, our parents would be attending a function, dressed in formal clothes.

Looking round the police station, I felt in another world. I couldn't believe that everything could be the same at home, while we waited for the superintendent, and Geoff Craig took our horses to be slaughtered. How could we go home and live normal lives again without Phantom and Killarney? It was unthinkable. I started to pace the room, screaming, "I can't stand it. I can't stand it any more . . ."

Dominic grabbed me. "Sit down, for goodness sake," he said. "Do you want to be locked up? Do you want to see a prison doctor?"

"A doctor would be better than no one," I answered bitterly.

"Shut up," said Angus. "You're hysterical."

"He's dying. Phantom's dying, they are killing him now. I feel it in my bones," I cried. "I shall never see him again, never. And it's your fault," I shouted at Angus. "He's dying because you wanted a moped."

"Calm down, miss," said the policeman. "The superintendent won't be long now."

"How long is long?" I cried.

"Ten minutes. Would you like some tea?"

We were brought cups of tea, and sausage rolls which tasted like sawdust in my mouth. It was now a quarter to two.

The weather had changed. We could hear rain

108

falling outside and the endless roar of traffic, quick footsteps, and voices complaining about the weather. And it was normal and sane; we were the only people out of step, sitting there accused of something we hadn't done.

Angus was talking to the policeman, explaining our situation, pointing at the clock, begging him to do something. Then Dominic started to sing, "Why are we waiting . . ." I shouted, "Phantom is dying while we wait. Have you hearts of stone? Do we look like vandals?"

Suddenly the waiting-room seemed full of police. In horror, I thought, they are going to lock us up, and knew there was no more hope.

A policewoman came towards me. I screamed, "We're innocent, please believe me. We don't break other people's things."

Angus was shouting, "You can't keep us here. It's against the law. We haven't done anything. We are law-abiding citizens. We have no prison records. You can't pin anything on us."

Then I heard a voice I knew. We all stopped shouting. It was Dad, striding across the room with dark shadows under his eyes, dressed in a suit, frightening in his rage, saying, "I want my children." The whole room seemed to clear and I saw that he had someone with him who must have been very high up, because the policeman called him 'sir'.

"Come out of here at once," said Dad, as though we had chosen to be there. "And get into the car. It's the Metro outside."

It was a strange car and Mum was inside, half crying, half laughing. I threw my arms around her neck and said, "They're killing Phantom."

"I know," she said. "We're going there next. We had to get you first."

Angus said, "I thought you were in Geneva," in a funny strained voice with a choke in it.

"We were, six hours ago," she replied.

As the rain beat against the windows I began to feel safe for the first time in hours.

Dad leapt into the car and cried, "Does anyone know the way?"

Dominic said, "I think so."

"Get in the front then," Dad shouted.

Two minutes later we were tearing through the town. There didn't seem any point in talking because there was only one thing which mattered now—to get to Geoff Craig's place in time.

Then Angus said, "I see you've got my tape-recorder."

Dad replied, "Yes, I played it to the Chief Constable."

I said, "You've been to the farm then?"

Mum nodded.

On the verges there were picnickers clearing up the remains of lunches, and in a field men were kicking a football. A church clock struck two and we overtook a party of tough young men on bicycles. The journey seemed to last forever. Dominic looked very tense, sitting up in front and trying to remember the way.

Mum said, "We were so frightened when you weren't at home. Then Mr Barnes telephoned. He said you were in a mess and we had better come back."

"I'm sorry," I said.

"You'll have to explain it all later," she said. "It

110

seems a bit of a mix-up. And what has happened to Angus's tooth?"

"We had a fight. It wasn't our fault," I answered, while all the time at the back of my mind Phantom was being killed, skinned, becoming just another carcass in the abattoir.

"It will have to be crowned," Mum said. "That will cost a fortune, but thank heavens you're safe."

"I'm to blame," announced Angus in a tight voice.

Then we saw the Land Rover parked in the layby, and Geoff Craig's farm. I started to pray.

"We're nearly there, sir," said Dominic. "That's his drive and his house, and the horses are in the hangar beyond."

"We're not going to fight," said Dad. "Don't get the wrong idea. We are acting within our rights. Let me deal with Mr Craig."

I was trying to see Phantom, but the yard was full of people and cars. I felt tired, too tired to see anything properly any more.

"Remember, no fighting," said Dad, as we turned up the drive. "Not even revenge if the horses are dead. You mustn't take the law into your own hands."

"I would like to murder June, but I won't," replied Angus.

"Who is she?"

"His daughter. Don't you know? I thought you knew everything," replied Angus.

I looked at Mum. Her face was lined with exhaustion. She was wearing a suit and the shoes which made her feet ache. Then I looked at the yard. There was no Phantom, just three police cars and Mr Barnes.

111

"Well done, Dad," shouted Dominic, as we all tumbled out of the car into the rain-soaked yard.

"They're questioning Mr Craig in the house. Are you all right son?" asked Mr Barnes.

I looked for Phantom again. I saw that the hangar doors were open.

"They had just taken a load when we arrived. I don't know if yours have gone," Mr Barnes told us. "We decided to see for ourselves what was going on."

We ran to the hangar.

"They will have taken Killarney for certain," said Angus.

The hangar was almost empty. Phantom stood tied up, soaked in sweat, with the weals from a whip fresh across his quarters, and blood on his hocks. He looked very sad with his head hanging low, and I knew he must have battled for a long time, but that somehow he had won. I put my arms round his neck and said, "It's all right, Phantom, you're going home." I couldn't look at Angus who stood, lost and alone in the hangar, looking for a horse which wasn't there. He seemed numb as he stood there, like someone who has fought long and hard and lost, and I had never seen so much remorse on anybody's face before.

Dominic came in and said, "They are arresting Geoff Craig. Are both your horses here?"

And then neither of us could look at Angus.

Dominic patted him on the shoulder and said, "No one could have done more."

I remembered that 'too late' and 'if only' are the saddest words in the English language, and wondered how long it would take Angus to recover from this moment.

I untied Phantom and said, "How can we get him home? He can't stay here another moment." Angus looked away, his eyes full of tears.

Then we heard a voice call, "Your horse is safe, Angus. I phoned the abattoir. He's coming back." And there was June, entering the hangar, red-eyed and somehow smaller with all her triumph gone.

"You saved him?" cried Angus.

"That's right. He was too good to go for meat," she answered, trying to make her voice sound matter-of-fact, when it was full of emotion.

"I said—take out the grey. He shouldn't be there, he's one of mine, there's been a terrible mistake," she told us.

"If you're being funny I'll kill you," said Angus.

"Listen, I can hear the box coming back. I have saved him for you, Angus. Be grateful . . ." she said.

I led Phantom out. There were only two policemen left in the yard. June's mother was talking to Mum. She looked very old, more like a granny than a mother.

"I knew something would happen one day, and I'm glad really. I can't stand the trade. I was always begging him to stop and so was June. Lots of people wouldn't speak to us because of it, they would cut us dead in the street, but I hope he doesn't go to prison," she said.

Angus stood waiting for the cattle truck, the awful despair gone from his face, while Dad talked to Mr Barnes about us.

Mum told me, "We kept ringing, Jean, but you were never there. We had to return. We were packing when Mr Barnes rang."

"Was Dad furious?" I asked.

113

"No, just upset. We caught the first plane we could. We found Mrs Parkin's message and there were no horses in the fields," continued Mum.

I could see it all in my mind's eye. I felt guilty.

"We forgot all about you," I said.

"And then your father telephoned the Chief Constable," explained Mum.

The cattle truck was coming up the drive.

"Did Mr Barnes play the recording?"

"Yes. But it didn't explain everything. You've still got a lot of explaining to do."

The truck stopped. Phantom lifted his tired head and whinnied. The ramp hit the concrete yard. Inside, Killarney was soaked in sweat.

Angus rushed forward.

"He knew where he was going, they always do, that's what makes it so horrible," said June.

Killarney was wearing a rope halter. He charged down the ramp and stared round the yard. He looked quite different, with nothing but fear on his face where once there had been wisdom.

"I suppose I should thank you," said Angus, looking at June.

She shook her head. "I should have spoken when I came to your house. I wanted to, but blood is thicker than water. Anyway, it's over now. I shall never ride again. Dad wanted me to go to the top. He wanted me to have everything he never had, but I often wished I had an ugly old cob which cost nothing. It would have been more fun that way."

"I know what you mean," replied Angus. "You wanted to do it the hard way, by yourself."

Killarney was dragging him down the drive,

desperately trying to get away from the Craig's place.

"I'm riding home," I said. "I can't bear another minute here."

"I'll fetch the trailer," replied Dominic.

"We can't wait. Thank you all the same," I said, vaulting on to Phantom. His sides were sticky with sweat.

"It's forty miles," said Mum.

"We can ride half-way. We can't stay here another minute. We must go," I answered. "The horses hate it. Look at them. Look at their eyes."

June was giving Angus a bridle. "Keep it," she said.

Dad was talking to the police.

"Dominic will fetch you," said Mr Barnes.

"Dominic has done enough," I answered.

"But someone must fetch you. You can't ride the whole way," said Mum.

The sky had cleared. I looked at the hangar and thought—no more horses will await their execution there.

Mum waved and shouted, "Go carefully."

"June has given me her tack," said Angus, riding alongside.

"She had a crush on you, goodness knows why," I answered.

"It's super. Look," continued Angus.

But I didn't want to look, for suddenly there was only one thing I wanted in the whole world, and that was to be in bed in Sparrow Cottage, with the birds singing outside and our horses grazing under the apple trees. I wanted to know that the nightmare was over. I wanted to wake up and be safe.

12

It was a long way home. Phantom hurried, but his stride had lost its swing. Every few yards he stumbled, his head was lower than usual, and I knew that for the first time in my life I was riding a truly exhausted horse.

I slid to the ground and straightened his mane; my legs felt weak and useless, and my eyes had stopped focussing properly again.

Angus dismounted slowly, his face pale, his right eye twitching. We didn't speak. We told our legs to walk and they walked. Right, left. Right, left. One, two. I tried to swing my arms, to be a soldier returning victorious from a long hard battle. I tried to sing, but I couldn't think of any words or any tune. My brain felt soft and soggy like cotton wool.

The police passed us slowly, obviously observing the Highway Code; then Mr Barnes, and Dominic, who wound down a window to shout, "We'll soon be back."

Our parents passed next, waving madly, Dad giving the thumbs-up sign.

Lights were going on in houses now. Children looked at us over gates and giggled. My tired legs continued to walk and my exhausted horse followed.

We reached a town. People stared. We must have looked strange—two tired figures followed by two tired horses with hardly a spark of life between us.

A man in a cap called, "What happened to you, then? Lost the fox, did you?"

We didn't answer. Lights shone on window displays. Shoppers jostled each other. Buses disgorged passengers. We didn't belong any more. We felt outside it all. As we waited at traffic-lights, with cars pressing our heels, a woman in a raincoat stepped forward.

"Here's an apple each for your horses," she said, taking them from a brown paper bag. "Are you all right? Is something wrong?"

"It was, but it's all right now," replied Angus.

"They were going to the abattoir. We were only just in time," I said, and saw the horror on her face as the lights changed.

I thought, she's nice, she understands, as a driver hooted and someone shouted, "You're holding us up."

Phantom dropped his apple but I couldn't stop to pick it up. Cars came from all directions, missing us by inches.

"It's the rush-hour," said Angus.

"That's no excuse," I answered.

Eventually we reached the suburbs. They looked leafy and empty after the town. The street lights came on.

"Dominic is being a long time," said Angus.

"It's a long way," I answered.

"I can't stand up much longer," said Angus. "I've never felt like this before."

"It's called exhaustion," I replied, giggling

feebly. "But at least we've won. I can't believe it ever happened now."

"What?" asked Angus.

"Everything."

My stomach was rumbling with hunger. Car lights blinded us. The suburbs ended, and night arrived with a dark, velvety sky.

"I hope we're going the right way," said Angus. "We've been walking on and on like zombies. Have you looked for signposts, because I haven't?"

I shook my head out of habit and said, "Supposing Dominic can't find us?"

"It will be a nuisance because we're tired. But it won't alter anything, because we've saved the horses, and that's all that matters," answered Angus.

There were now grass verges on either side of the road, and with one accord we collapsed on to a bank and let our horses graze.

"I am going to give Killarney to Dominic," announced Angus. "I don't need him. I am going across Europe on a bicycle. And he deserves something."

"On a bicycle?" I repeated. "But when?"

"This summer. Dominic likes you," continued Angus. "You can ride together. You won't miss me."

"We're only good friends," I answered, but I knew it wasn't true. I liked him too. It could even be love, but I wasn't sure, not yet anyway. "I feel safe with him," I continued. "I know he can change a wheel or throw an enemy over his shoulder. I don't have to worry when I am with him."

Suddenly we could see the lights of a Land Rover.

"They're coming, they're here," cried Angus, standing up, and we waved tired arms, our horses raised tired heads and stared.

"It's all right this time," I told Phantom. "We're going home."

Dominic stepped out of the Land Rover and let down the ramp on the trailer.

"You're on the wrong road," he said in an exasperated voice. "We thought we would never find you."

I knew that Dominic would never be on the wrong road, because he would always have the right maps, or would look at the right signposts, because he's that sort of person.

Angus said, "I'm sorry. We just kept walking. You know us, Dominic."

And he sighed and said, "I should by now, shouldn't I? But I still like you, that's what's so funny."

Phantom walked into the trailer after me, but Killarney stopped and started to shake in every limb.

"Oh no!" cried Angus. "He's never going to box again."

"He thinks he's going to the abattoir, poor old fellow," replied Mr Barnes, fetching a bucket of oats from the trailer.

We lifted his hooves one by one on to the ramp. We talked to him. We pushed him from behind. We coaxed and wheedled, until only Mr Barnes was steady on his legs and the rest of us were shaking with exhaustion.

"Mother's put some sandwiches and a Thermos

of coffee in the Land Rover. Go and eat. Leave him to me," said Mr Barnes.

We ate in silence, too tired for words.

"We've won, you realise that, don't you?" asked Angus after a time. "Geoff Craig will never sell horses to an abattoir again."

I nodded. We could hear Killarney's hooves walking into the trailer and Mr Barnes talking in a soothing voice, praising him. The coffee revived us.

"Well done, Dad," said Dominic.

Mr Barnes started the engine. He smelt of tobacco. The day seemed to have lasted a thousand years.

"Go to sleep," said Mr Barnes. "There's nothing to worry about now."

The heater was on in the Land Rover and the next thing I knew was that we were home. Dad let down the ramp. Mum said, "There's supper waiting."

Phantom backed out, looked round and gave a sigh of pure contentment. The orchard looked beautiful beyond words in the moonlight which had appeared while we slept.

"We don't know how to thank you, Mr Barnes," began Dad.

"I don't need any thanks," he said.

Dominic leant on the yard gate.

"Perhaps we'll see more of you now, Jean," he suggested.

"Without a doubt," I answered.

Phantom was rolling, his legs silver in the moonlight, while Killarney looked at the orchard as though seeing it for the first time.

"I'm fetching them feeds," said Angus.

"Hang on, there are some carrots inside," cried Mum, running to the cottage.

"I'm going to pay for the petrol," announced Dad.

"Don't be silly," replied Mr Barnes, getting into the Land Rover and slamming the door.

"I'll see you, then," said Dominic.

"Thank you for everything," I answered. "You saved us and our horses. We owe everything to you." It sounded more dramatic than I meant, because suddenly I felt overwhelmed by the events of the day.

"We would be dead if you hadn't helped," I added.

"Don't be idiotic," answered Dominic, walking towards the Land Rover.

"Our horses would be, anyway," I replied. "And you can't deny that!"

Angus had two buckets of feed in his hands. "I think they are better out, don't you?" he asked.

I looked at the sky. It was still dark and velvety, without a cloud to be seen.

"Yes. They've been shut in long enough," I answered.

We went across the orchard together. Our horses lifted their heads and whinnied, their ordeal over. Phantom pushed me with his head and sighed again before plunging his nose into the bucket.

They are home, I thought. And horses need homes too.

Mum was calling, "Supper." We could see the lights of the Barnes's Land Rover bumping along the lane to the farm.

"You can't sell Killarney, not ever," I said.

"Only lend or give," answered Angus. "And you know to whom . . ."

Dad stood in the doorway calling, "Will you come in at once."

And then it was like any other evening. Our nightmare was over. We were home, tired but triumphant. I stopped to listen to Phantom munching before I went inside, and it was one of the most wonderful sounds I had ever heard, better than all the pop songs in the world. All I wanted was to sleep and to wake up in the morning and know that our horses were still here, and that Phantom would live here until he died.

But I knew it would not be that easy—nothing ever is.

Other titles in
THE PHANTOM HORSE series
£1.95

No. 1 Phantom Horse
No. 2 Phantom Horse Comes Home
No. 3 Phantom Horse Goes To Ireland
No. 5 Phantom Horse Goes To Scotland
No. 6 Wait For Me Phantom Horse